THE HEALING TOUCH

Written by

Tita Horvat

Author: Tita Horvat
Title: The Healing Touch
Publisher: Tita Horvat

www.amazon.com, www.lulu.com, www.titaslife.com
1st edition, Ljubljana 2017

Some characters and events in this publication are based on real people and events, while others are fictitious and any resemblance to real persons, living or dead, is purely coincidental.

CIP - Kataložni zapis o publikaciji
Narodna in univerzitetna knjižnica, Ljubljana
821.163.6-311.2

HORVAT, Tita
The healing touch / written by Tita Horvat. - 1st ed. - Ljubljana : [selfpublisher] T. Horvat, 2017

ISBN 978-961-94117-9-7
COBISS.SI-ID 288878080

This book is dedicated to my dear sisters, who have been my rock and source of unconditional love for many years.

Table of Contents

Chapter 1

Relaxing summer days seem nothing but a distant memory now even though I only got back to work a few days ago. I enjoy the freedom summer holidays bring with them – getting up when your body is completely rested, not having to rush breakfast, then going to the gym, having a home-cooked meal, spending time in the sun in the afternoon, and meeting up with friends for drinks or dinner in the evening. Pure heaven!

This doesn't mean that I don't like my job – on the contrary, I love it, but sometimes it just gets too hectic, like any other job. Quite often I need to remind myself to slow down and just live in the moment. I have even set a reminder on my mobile phone in case I get too caught up in work.

Another thing I don't particularly enjoy about my job is seminars. In fact, this is the worst way to start off a new school year, and yet here I am, sitting in the teacher conference room, somewhat listening to what is being said. Luckily, the presenter is coming to the end of her seminar.

'Any abuse, be it verbal, physical, sexual, or emotional, that we experience in childhood can have lasting consequences, and that is why we must have zero tolerance for it.'

Child abuse is never an easy subject to talk about, but we teachers deal with it quite often. It's even more personal for me because I grew up with an abusive mother. What I've learnt is that while hits hurt during the abuse and a few days after it, words hurt for years and years. Although you don't believe they are true when you hear them and are defying them inside your mind and soul when you hear someone say them to you, over time, when you hear them often, they slip into your brain and slowly replace all the nice things you hear and believe about yourself until there is nothing else but low self-esteem and a great yearning to be loved. That is why I decided to become a teacher who finds good things about her pupils and says them out loud often because children need to hear praises often so that they can see that they *are* capable and worthy.

It's still hard for me to understand why my mum would only pick on me and my older sister, but never say a bad word about my younger one. I could never really figure out what Maya had that made mum love her, and what was it that she detested so much in me. So, as a child I would be jealous of Maya, but never to a point that I would hate her. In fact, my two sisters were the ones I could rely on, they offered me comfort and love. Even now, 20 years later, we are still our greatest supporters.

My colleagues start clapping and I am back in present time. One of my best friends, Petra, is sitting next to me. We met at college, and our friendship grew stronger and stronger. Petra is from California, and this made my decision to stay and search for a job here that much easier.

'Do you want to grab some lunch? Last relaxing lunch before the new school year begins?' asks Petra.

'I'd love to, but I have some leftovers from last night. How about brunch tomorrow at 11?'

It's a lovely warm and sunny afternoon, so I decide to walk home from work. There's nothing better after a stressful day than to walk the streets and just observe people passing by, seeing them smile and making up nice stories about what made them feel like this. You can see that the simplest things bring people the greatest pleasures – eating ice cream on a hot day, playing catch with your dog, holding hands with your loved ones, talking about your day or making plans for a weekend getaway with your best friend, or just hearing your favorite song on the radio while shopping.

I am so absorbed in this that I almost walk past a pet shop. Luckily, a girl and her dog walk out of it and I remember that I need to buy some dog biscuits because I have run out of them.

Mr. Jones, the shop owner, is one of the nicest people I've ever met, and like always he greets me with a smile.

'Hi, Tina. Have you already run out of the biscuits?'

'Hello, Mr. Jones. What can I say - there are a lot of dogs in my neighborhood that need some pampering.'

'Do you want the usual ones?'

'Yes, I just love how nice they smell.'

Vanilla is my favorite scent, and if you hold the biscuits in your hands for a couple of minutes, you can still smell them hours later. Years ago, when I first came across them, I was really tempted to try one, just to see if they taste as wonderful as they smell, but the list of ingredients put me off that idea. Nonetheless, dogs love them, so they must be good.

Mr. Jones hands me the biscuits, and just as I am getting my purse out, he surprises me.

'These are on me.'

'Oh, that is really sweet of you. Thank you!'

As I said, he is really nice. I take out some coins from my wallet and put them into a donations box on the counter. The local animal shelter needs all the donations they can get.

'Have a wonderful day!' I say to Mr. Jones and wave goodbye.

'You too!'

I wait until I get out of the shop and then I open the bag, smell the content and smile. Why can't our biscuits smell like this? I guess it's because then we wouldn't want to stop eating them and we'd put on tremendous amount of weight and get really unhealthy.

I put some of them inside my jacket pocket just to have them with me when I don't bring my purse, and put the rest of the bag inside my purse.

When I decided to stay in California, I was thinking about sharing an apartment with Petra. While it would be fun to have someone around 24/7, we both decided that it was best if each had our own place, just because this would allow us do our own things when and how we wanted. I, for one thing, love sleeping in at the weekend, and when I say sleeping in, I mean sleeping until nine or ten, while Petra sets her alarm clock even at the weekends. Crazy, ha? I mean, who does that? She thinks this is best because this way her body has a routine. Not getting enough sleep, or being hungry, makes me cranky, so basically having my own apartment makes me a nicer person. Petra and I can always meet up, have sleepovers, and do silly girly things, it just isn't every day.

I really lucked out when I found the apartment. It's in a relatively quiet neighborhood, with lots of greenery, the neighbors are amazing, there's a gym within walking distance, and shops and cafés are also relatively near. The apartment itself is a perfect size – there's a nice bedroom, a bathroom, a spacious kitchen, a dining room, and a lovely living room. I immediately fell in love with the modern design of the furniture and the little things like cute pillows, lovely vases, and interesting shelving units that make it more homey and inviting.

Another good thing is that the apartment building has got an elevator. While I consider myself an active person, I do find it a blessing when I don't have to carry grocery bags up to the third floor or, like now, when I am too tired to walk up all those stairs.

My stomach begins growling and I think to myself that it's great that I don't have to cook because I have some leftovers in the fridge. My floor can't come soon enough. The elevator door opens, and a dog starts barking.

I get startled but not because I am afraid of dogs, but because I wasn't expecting there to be a dog on my floor. None of my neighbors have one.

It's a beautiful Golden Retriever, and I know that they are pretty harmless, so I bend down and put my hand in front of it, back side of my hand facing the dog's nose so that it can get acquainted with me.

'Oh, hello there, you pretty little thing,' I say in a sweet and calming voice.

A man is standing behind the dog and is pulling the leash back.

'Shhh! No. Stop barking.'

I can't really see him properly because I am bent down.

Luckily, the dog calms down. Perhaps it can smell the vanilla from the dog biscuits on my hand.

'You weren't expecting anyone to be in the elevator, now were you?' I say. I lift my head slightly and look at the man. He is tall, with short brown hair, a nice tan, and very good-looking. He seems to be in his late twenties and is dressed casually as you would normally be when taking the dog out.

'Is it OK if I give her a dog biscuit?' I ask him.

'Sure.'

I take a dog biscuit out of my pocket and give it to the dog.

'You see, I am not a terrible person,' I say in a friendly voice. I lift my head. 'What's …' I start and quickly look if it is a male or a female, '… her name?'

'Goldie,' he replies. He has a nice voice. Relatively deep, but friendly.

'Oh, because she's a golden retriever, right? That's cute,' I say and smile. 'How old is she?'

'3 years.'

'So she has just started obeying you.'

We both smile. He has a really lovely smile, and I've always been a sucker for those. I know that most people go for the eyes or the hands, but for me smile is the important one. When he smiled, his eyes smiled too, and they both exuded warmth.

The dog pulls the man past me and inside the elevator.

'I guess she really needs to go,' he says, half apologetically.

'You must never keep a lady waiting,' I reply with a half serious face. 'Bye.'

'Bye.'

The elevator door closes and I go to my apartment, ready to devour dinner.

Chapter 2

I wake up at 10 the next morning, which is pretty late by my standards, but this always happens after the first week back at work. Luckily, I have an hour before I am meeting Petra for brunch. I decide to do some stretching exercises to kill time and then I walk to the café.

Petra is already sitting down. Ah, teachers and their punctuality! But I must admit I hated being late (and someone else being late) even before I became a teacher.

We often eat at this café, so I don't even look at the menu when the waiter takes my order. All of their food is amazing – it's the kind you'd wish for your last meal.

Petra gives out a sigh and says, 'I'm going to miss relaxing days and lazy weekends.'

'Me too. But it's great to be surrounded by young energy again.'

'Hey, are you calling me old?' She tries to look offended as she says it, but there's a smile there, so I know she is joking.

'You know what I mean.' Of course I don't consider us old, I mean, we are only in our twenties, but there is something special about being surrounded by children and their energy, their outlook on life and just pure joy. It definitely keeps you young.

'I know,' she replies with a smile.

After a brief silence, she becomes serious and a bit hesitant. 'Listen, I was thinking. You are single, and I am single, so why don't we …'

‘Get together?’ I cut her speech with a naughty smile on my face.

‘Ha, ha, very funny. I mean, you *are* attractive, and let’s face it so am I, but I still prefer men, and so do you. Or has something changed?’ she asks with a suspicious look.

‘No, still the same,’ I reply.

I must admit that in general I find a woman’s body a lot more beautiful than a man’s, but I’ve only been attracted to men. Sounds strange, I know, but that’s how it is.

‘So, what I was thinking is … we should try speed dating,’ she says carefully.

‘Oh, god, please, no,’ I say as if she suggested something outrageous. Just the thought of dating sends shivers down my spine. I’ve never been quite successful in that department and I’ve had my fair share of heartbreaks, just enough to make me not want to do it again in the near future.

‘What have you got to lose? You can’t just work all the time, you have to make time for some play,’ she tries to convince me.

‘But I do go out!’ I start to object.

I can see that Petra is getting really excited at hearing me say this.

‘Really?’ she asks with a surprised tone in her voice.

‘I mean I do go out in public. I go to the gym three times a week,’ I reply proudly, hoping this would put an end to the subject.

‘The last time I checked that hasn’t brought you a date.’

‘True, but ...’ I try to object even though I know she is right.

‘You can’t just expect Prince Charming to knock on your door and say, ‘Hi, Tina, I am your Prince Charming. Now, let’s get married.’

‘You never know. These things happen,’ I reply, but you can hear it in my tone that even I don’t believe in it.

‘Yeah, in movies.’

‘They can happen in real life,’ I reply with a slight defying tone in my voice. And then I add a quiet, ‘Maybe just not as often as in movies.’

Petra sighs and smiles. I smile back.

The waiter brings us our order, and Petra tucks right in, while I just can’t stop thinking about what we’ve just been talking about. It’s true that such things mostly happen in movies while in real life things are more complicated and not every story has a happy ending, but the romantic in me just can’t let go of the notion. Surely it can happen that one day you meet someone special while walking your dog or by just bumping into them at a store or in your apartment building. Who is to say that the cute guy with the golden retriever …

‘You’ve got that dreamy look in your eyes,’ I hear Petra say. ‘Is there something I don’t know?’

‘No,’ I sort of lie.

‘Tina!?’ she says, questioning my answer. Maybe because my voice went slightly up at the end. I should have made it seem more like a statement but I’ve never been good at lying. I guess it’s time to come clean.

‘Well, yesterday, I saw this cute guy in my apartment building. We only talked for a second, so I can’t really say anything about him.’

‘How do you know he wasn’t just visiting his girlfriend?’

Yup, she sure knows how to knock the daydreaming romantic out of me. Aren’t friends supposed to be there for each other?

‘Because there are only older couples on my floor. And I know that the couple from 3B moved out last month, and last week I saw people bringing in some new furniture, so I am guessing he lives there now.’

‘Maybe he moved in with his girlfriend.’

‘That’s probably true, considering my luck in love.’ I let out a sigh.

‘Anyway, I think we need to try speed dating. My cousin’s best friend found a girlfriend through speed dating and they’ve been together for half a year now.’

There’s always a friend’s friend or a cousin’s high school boyfriend’s sister who is involved in these stories, isn’t there? It makes you wonder if there’s any truth to them.

‘You’re really twisting my arm here. I hate you.’ My face expression matches how I feel about these things. But I give in. ‘Ugh, when is it and how long does it last?’

‘I don’t know, it’ll be my first time. I’ll check when I get home.’

Hopefully, she’ll forget all about it by the time she gets there.

Chapter 3

Ah, Friday afternoon – the most anticipated and loved moment of the whole week. Pupils agree with me because as soon as the school bell rings, they get out of the classroom. And who could blame them?

As I am clearing my desk, I hear a knock at the door. It's Petra, slightly tired, but she still manages a smile.

'Survived the first week?' she asks with a wink.

'They are actually really nice and well-behaved.' I guess I really lucked out this year, but you can never really be too sure. 'How's your class?'

'I have a couple of rowdy ones but I've got some tricks up my sleeve.'

We both smile. She always has at least one pupil in her class who wants to test boundaries, but she's really good at calming them down and making sure that they settle in nicely without disrupting the others.

'Listen,' she says with an apologetic tone, 'I know I promised that I would start going to the gym this year, but I don't think I can make it today.'

This is so like her – she's never been particularly fond of working out and would always promise to come with me, and to be fair she did come a couple of times, but she just never seems to stick with it for longer than one month. Oh, and did you notice she said 'this year' and what she meant was 'this school year'? That's teachers for you.

‘Why? Have you got papers to grade?’ I joke. No one gives their pupils a test the first week of school no matter how strict a teacher they are.

‘No, but I … I …’

I stop her before she can think of an excuse. ‘No buts, you are coming and that’s it! New school year, new you, remember? Besides, you’ll feel amazing afterwards.’

She frowns and says, ‘OK, but promise to be gentle. It’ll be my first time in a long time.’

‘I promise. I’ll see you at 6 then.’

I rush home so I have time for a quick snack and a shower. No one wants to work out next to a stinker.

Since the gym is within a walking distance, I put my gym clothes on. It’s nothing fancy, just some leggings and a top. I’ve always been more comfort-over-style kind of girl, and I believe that sports clothes can pass as regular clothes as long as you wear a slightly longer top when running around town. I even have one part of the wardrobe dedicated to sports clothes – that way I don’t accidentally wear them to work.

I still have some minutes to spare, so I grab a towel, socks, trainers, and a water bottle and put them in my gym bag and I am out of my apartment.

As I am closing the door, I hear a door open, and that handsome man and Goldie get out of their apartment. He is still as gorgeous as the day I met him. Goldie runs towards me, wagging her tail. It’s so nice to know she remembers me from last week but that’s golden retrievers for you – give them some food and you’ll be in their hearts forever. I quickly take a few dog biscuits from the shelf by the door and lock the door.

I notice that another man in his early 30s is standing at the door. He is slightly taller than my cute neighbor and has blond hair. They hug, say 'I love you' to each other, and then the blond man closes the door.

Bummer! I guess that solves the mystery then. While it's nice to know that he lives here, it's terrible that my cute neighbor is gay. Don't get me wrong, I have nothing against homosexuals – hey, I've got a gay nephew whom I adore – but this is definitely not the news I accept with a smile on my face.

Goldie barks, so I turn my attention to her.

'Oh, hello, Miss G. How are you today?' I pat her head, and then she immediately starts sniffing my hand to see if there's a snack for her there. 'I know, I know, you want a biscuit.'

I smile and give her the biscuit I took off my shelf, and then I remember that I forgot to ask for permission. Some dog owners are strongly against other people giving treats to their dogs, so I put on my remorseful face and say, 'Oh, sorry, I forgot to ask if it was OK to give her one.'

Luckily, he takes it lightly.

'It's fine,' he replies and waves his hand. 'Besides, who could resist her puppy eyes?'

A sense of relief goes over me and I smile to him.

'True, they have that mastered to perfection.'

He smiles back, and it still is one of the most beautiful smiles I've ever seen.

'I don't think I've introduced myself. I'm David,' he says and offers me his hand.

'Tina. Nice to meet you,' I say as I shake his hand. His grip is strong and gentle at the same time, and his hand is relatively soft for a man's hand. Of course, what else could you expect from a gay man? They generally take care of themselves much more than straight men, and I love that about them.

Goldie runs towards the elevator and we follow her.

'So, how do you like it here?' I ask. I hope he likes it a lot and wants to stay for a very long time.

'I really like the neighborhood. There's so much to do. And the neighbors are also nice.'

'Has Mrs. Williams already brought you her famous and delicious apple pie?'

She makes the most wonderful pies I have ever tasted and she always greets new neighbors with one of her pies. I once suggested her to start selling them but she refused, telling me it would take the fun out of baking if she had to do it every day and in large quantities.

'A couple of days ago,' he replies. Then he starts smiling and adds, 'and another one this morning.'

She must really like him and who could blame her. 'Ah, bless her. She's really nice. She's just a bit lonely ever since her husband died last year.'

Her husband was also nice and he would always lend a helping hand if something broke down and the repairman wasn't available for some time.

We come out of the apartment building and are greeted by the warm sun.

Being a helpful neighbor, I point to my right and say, 'I don't know if you've already been there but if you walk two blocks in this direction and then turn right, you should come to a nice dog park.'

'That's great. Thank you.'

'It's not hard to find.'

My phone starts ringing and I know without even looking at it that it's Petra.

'I must be going,' I say as I am searching for the phone in my gym bag. 'A friend is waiting for me. Have a nice day! Bye!'

'Bye.'

I pet Goldie goodbye, then wave to David, and we go in opposite directions.

It only takes me a few minutes to get to the gym and I actually manage to get there on time, so teachers' worst fear doesn't materialize.

Petra is standing at the entrance door in her workout clothes, so we are in the gym in no time, carrying a towel and a bottle in our hands.

'What do we do first?' she asks and looks around the gym. It seems quite empty today, which is great because you don't have to wait for your turn at the machines.

I point to the warm-up area. 'Let's warm up. I don't want you to call in sick because you can't get out of bed.'

Not that it's ever happened and this also won't happen because it's Saturday tomorrow, but I say it anyway.

'Hey, you promised you'd go easy on me, remember?'

'Don't worry, I will,' I reassure her.

The gym is relatively new and has all the equipment you need. What I really like about it is that the treadmills, the elliptical trainers, and the stationary bikes have a built-in fan so you can keep cool while working out. The gym has a proper air conditioning as well, but it doesn't help much when you are doing a HIIT. After warming up we go to stationary bikes and start biking.

'So, have you given speed dating any thought?' Petra surprises me.

'Not really,' I reply and it's the absolute truth. I try to push the unpleasant things to the place in my mind that is hard to get to.

'Tina!?' she almost yells out.

'But I guess I will have to go,' I reply with a face expression that shows I've given in as well as that I don't like the idea. 'It turns out that the cute guy that has just moved into my apartment building is gay.'

‘Oh, bummer, that’s even worse than having a girlfriend because then you at least stand a chance,’ she replies with an upset face. And she is completely right.

I can only manage to say, ‘Such is life, I guess.’ With my dating history I am kind of used to the universe having something against me finding love.

Petra is already thinking about our next step. ‘I will sign us up as soon as I get home. If I remember correctly, there’s one next weekend.’

‘Plenty of time to mentally prepare for it, then.’

‘Ah, it can’t be that bad.’

‘We’ll see.’ But she might be right. I’ve never been to speed dating, so I shouldn’t really be so negative about it. It might be fun. ‘And who knows, if you start going to the gym more often, you might meet someone here,’ I add.

She’s never had trouble with meeting men. She is tall, with long luscious brown hair, captivating green-grey eyes, and a warm smile – men just have to take one look at her and they’re head over heals. Even though she is gorgeous, men aren’t afraid to approach her – I guess they see she has that easy-going and nice energy around her.

‘Yeah, I don’t know about that. I’m not such a fitness freak.’

Just as I want to reply, a man in his early 30s with big muscles walks past. I can see that Petra’s eyes follow him, and then she turns to me and says in a quiet voice, ‘But I might have just got the push that I needed.’

We both start laughing but quietly because we don't want the man to think we are making fun of him.

'I am starting to understand why you spend lots of time here,' she says while still laughing.

'I don't do it for that. I come here to de-stress and keep active,' I reply with a serious face. I am being sincere.

But she objects to my answer, saying, 'Yeah, yeah.'

I put on my serious face. 'Half of the time I don't even notice there are people here.' This might be a small lie, because I do notice them, but I usually just admire their sculpted physique and then I have a look at their exercise routines and incorporate them into my routine.

'Really?' she replies with a surprised look on her face. Then she leans in and almost whispers, 'I mean, just look at all the fit men.'

I cannot but smile at her comment, but I still reply with, 'I guess I've never found really muscular men that attractive.' I'm sure I'm not the only woman who thinks so. I do like a man who takes care of himself, but I definitely prefer a lean and toned body to a super muscular one.

'You're weird.'

'One of us has to be,' I reply with a smile on my face. 'Enough chatting, let's get down to some real work.'

I start pedaling faster and Petra follows my lead.

Chapter 4

Another week has passed. Petra's been a good girl - she came with me to the gym on Wednesday and she promised to come tomorrow as well. A miracle, I know!

The weather continues to spoil us, but that is almost always the case in California, so I shouldn't be surprised. Since the week hasn't been that stressful, I decide to skip the gym and go for a walk.

I take off my dress, put on leggings and a cute top, fill the bottle with coconut water, and I am good to go. It seems that David and Goldie have the same agenda because they are standing at the elevator door.

'Hi. Going to the gym?' David asks while Goldie greets me with wagging her tail.

'No, just a walk this time.' I guess he doesn't see that I don't have my gym bag with me, or maybe he doesn't take one with him when he goes to the gym.

'Then join us. Goldie always behaves better around you.'

'The magic of dog biscuits,' I reply with a wink and a smile. Goldie is sitting between us and looking up at us, almost smiling. It seems as if she understands what we are talking about.

A minute later we are walking along the street.

'How was the dog park I told you about last week?' I ask him.

'Goldie loved it. I think we were there for two hours and she had to take a nap afterwards.'

'Poor girl! But it's nice that dogs can have a place where they don't have to be on a leash,' I say.

'I agree. I always think how it would make *me* feel if the roles were reversed.'

A man who has empathy, what more could you ask for? For him to be straight, I guess.

'Yeah, dogs need to be able to run freely. It keeps them active, fit, and young. The same is true for people.'

'My agent would agree with you,' he replies with a smile.

'Oh, are you an actor?' I ask, and in my head I add 'Or a model?'

'Guilty,' he replies, half apologetically.

'Have I seen you in anything?' I don't think I have because I'm sure I would remember him. I have a pretty selective memory – while I have trouble with remembering my pupils' names even though I see them every day, I can immediately tell if I've seen a cute actor before, even if years have passed. Take Matt Bomer – I first saw him in a TV series called Tru Calling where he played a minor part, but when I saw him in White Collar about six years later, I immediately knew I had seen him before! What's even weirder is that I remembered the exact scene I had seen him first in Tru Calling.

He shakes his head. 'I've mostly done small parts and commercials, so I guess not.'

'Well, you never know when you'll get that big break,' I try to encourage him.

'I'm not complaining as long as it pays the bills,' he replies but something in his reply and facial expression tells me that he would love to have a bigger role. 'And what do you do? Are you a personal trainer?' he asks me.

I laugh out loud. It's the first time anyone has ever said I look like a professional trainer, because I don't think I do – my muscles are definitely not that big that would qualify me for one.

'No, but I guess you'd think so since you've seen me in workout clothes on several occasions,' I finally manage to say. 'Actually, I'm a teacher.'

'I wouldn't have guessed.' The surprised look that accompanies this suggests that he really wouldn't have.

'I guess sometimes looks can be deceiving.'

People often don't believe it when I say that I'm a teacher. I guess I don't have a teacher vibe, whatever that is. Perhaps it's because I don't carry a briefcase with me? I simply prefer doing everything work-related at work so that home is my relaxation zone. I don't always succeed – mainly during the exam time, but I am getting there.

'So, what kind of a teacher are you?'

I don't even have to think about my answer. 'I've always admired my teachers who were strict but fair so that is what I aim for.'

'My high school Math teacher was like that.'

'And you still hate him or her,' I joke with a serious face.

'No, nothing like that.' The way he says it makes me think he took my joke seriously. I must remember to add a wink next time I joke like that. Before I can tell him that I was only joking, he continues, 'I will admit that back then I did wish he gave us easier tests but looking back I realize that he taught us a lot – also about life.'

'That's nice to hear.' Finally, someone who understands.

We walk past the gym I go to.

'Oh, this is the gym I go to.'

'Are you trying to say that all those pies that Mrs. Williams has brought are showing?' he replies and looks down at his stomach.

'No, you look great,' I quickly respond. Maybe too quickly, so I add, 'I just thought you might want to get your agent off your back.'

'Speaking of food, how come you always have some dog biscuits with you?'

Oh, no, the question I dread the most, and it's not because it's malicious or because it would require me to come up with some lie, but because I really miss my dog and I'm just trying not to get too emotional when I have to answer it.

'Well, I used to have a dog, and I would carry treats for her in my pocket and I also gave them to the dogs we'd meet in the dog park. There's nothing better than seeing a dog running towards you with a smile on their face because they know you have something for them.' Wow, it's the first time I've managed to say it without getting tear-eyed.

‘So, you bribed them,’ he replies with a smile.

‘In a way. And I guess that even though she’s gone, I still want to make their day, so I continue to carry biscuits with me.’

‘Aww, that’s really nice.’

We continue walking for about an hour, talking about funny things that we’ve experienced at our job and about everyday things.

Chapter 5

The dreaded day of speed dating has finally arrived. I don't know why I am so reluctant to try it out. I've seen it in quite a few movies and series and I have laughed at some situations, so I should be excited to see if those situations actually happen in real life. And besides, you only have to spend a few minutes with a man, so how hard can it be?

So here I am, standing in front of my wardrobe, trying to choose the best outfit. The last thing I heard Petra say to me was, 'Make an effort!' and now I am panicking. What do you wear that is still you but that men also find attractive? All the dresses that I have obviously haven't worked their magic, so I decide to phone Petra.

Before I can say anything, she says, 'You're coming and that's it.'

'Hello to you, too,' I greet her. 'I'm just phoning to ask if you have anything in your wardrobe that I could borrow for tonight.'

'I think I could find a few things that would look great on you. I'll be there in half an hour.'

'But nothing too revealing or too short, please!' I add and hope that she heard it.

Twenty minutes later she is at my door. She looks amazing! She is wearing a dress with an animal print, but it doesn't look sleazy which often happens with this print. She is wearing contact lenses and her make up is perfect. The earrings match the dress and add a sparkle to her eyes.

I show her the dresses that I was thinking of wearing, but she doesn't seem that impressed by them. She takes out a green dress with a beautiful pattern and a V-neck. I have my doubts, but they disappear when I put it on.

'Wow, I look quite nice in it,' I say with a surprised look on my face.

'Now, let's make your eyes shine,' she adds and takes an eyeshadow palette from her bag.

Twenty minutes later, we are in the restaurant where the speed dating will be taking place. A woman in her mid-30s approaches us.

'Hello! My name is Ann,' she says and extends her hand. 'I'm the organizer.'

We introduce ourselves, and Ann asks us if this is our first time at speed dating. I guess it's easy to spot newcomers because they don't know what to – should they sit down, and if yes, where, should they start talking with others, etc.

She gives us our name tags and each has a number on it. We clip them on, and then Ann takes us to a table and explains, 'You sit at the table with the same number as on your name tag. The ladies get to sit down the whole time and the men rotate. You then have 7 minutes to talk to each other, and if you run out of ideas of what to talk about, there's a cheat sheet on the table.'

I'm guessing Petra hasn't seen a movie with a speed dating scene, because she asks, 'How do we know when the 7 minutes are up?'

Ann must have heard this question a million times, yet she is very calm and friendly when she replies, 'I will ring this bell,' and takes a bell from the table and rings it. She takes a piece of paper from the table, shows it to us and says, 'There's a piece of paper and a pen on the table so that you can write down the names of the men and then circle 'Yes' if you want to go on a second date or 'No' if you aren't interested. At the end of speed dating, you will give it to me so I can see if you got any matches, and then you can expect an email from me in a couple of days with email addresses of men who also showed an interest in you.'

Lots of information, but we manage to take it all in.

Ann turns and takes us to the table that has welcome drinks on them. There's water, orange juice, wine, and some cocktails – I guess that sometimes you need some liquid courage, but I still opt for orange juice. I've never really been much of a drinker – I once started getting dizzy after a couple of sips of Bacardi Breezer (it contained 5% alcohol) and I usually get really hot just after one sip, so I think that my body cannot tolerate alcohol. Petra, on the other hand, loves wine. She wasn't much of a drinker either, but her last boyfriend loved wine and ever since Petra drinks it occasionally.

After a few minutes, we hear Ann's voice, 'Ladies and gentlemen, please take your seats, and let the fun begin.'

I must admit that the first couple of conversations are quite nerve-racking, at least on my part, and I do have to look at the cheat sheet with a couple of men. After some time, I start getting a slight headache and I feel quite tired, so I am relieved when I hear Ann ring a bell and say, 'This is the end of round one. We will have a short break now and then continue with part two.'

Men and women stand up and walk towards the bar area, and I go over to Petra's table.

‘This is terrible,’ I say with a painful expression on my face.

‘Come one, it can’t be that bad,’ she replies. I’m surprised how she doesn’t seem as tired as I am.

I give evidence to my statement and tell her about my dates so far, well, about the horrible ones, at least, ‘There’s a guy who didn’t ask me anything and his only reply to my questions was Yes or No. I swear it made me feel like I was at work – he was a pupil who hadn’t really studied and I was trying to get at least something out of him to give him a D.’

Petra starts laughing, and I continue, ‘The longest 7 minutes of my life, I’m telling you. Oh, and then there was another one who checked me out at the end when he got up. He stood up, came closer, and then looked at my figure from the neck to my feet. It made me feel like a piece of meat.’

Petra gives a genuine disgusted look and says, ‘That’s terrible.’

‘Can we just leave?’ I beg her. I try my best puppy eyes but I don’t think they are working because she starts walking towards other men and women, who are chatting at the bar area.

‘I would say yes, but do you see that cute guy?’ she says and points at a man with her head. ‘He hasn’t been at my table yet and I want to know what he’s like.’

I give out a deep sigh and say, ‘The sacrifices I make for you.’

‘Besides, there are some normal guys coming up,’ she tries to cheer me up. ‘In fact, there’s one that I think you might like.’

She succeeds in getting my attention. I look around and ask, ‘Which one?’

But just as she is about to show me, a waiter approaches us and asks, 'What can I get you, ladies?'

Round two is slightly better than round one, but I am still very happy when it's over. As Petra and I are walking down the street after speed dating, I beg her, 'Promise me you'll never make me do it again.'

All that Petra can manage is, 'I promise I will give you a break of a few weeks.'

'Petra!?' I protest. 'I think I need a drink or a night out after this.'

Petra seems excited at my proposal, 'Dancing all night long? Sounds perfect.'

We start walking faster when I gasp in surprise, stop, and turn around. Petra asks me what's wrong and I point my head towards two men and almost whisper, 'Do you see those two men kissing?'

Petra seems bewildered by my statement because her 'Yes, so?' has that tone that conveys 'There's nothing wrong with that. What on Earth are you upset about?'

I whisper my explanation, 'One of them is David's boyfriend.'

Petra looks confused and asks, 'Who's David?'

'My neighbor, you know, that cute one,' I say, with stress on 'cute'.

At first, Petra smiles, I guess it's because I said I find David cute, but then she realizes what this means and gives out a sad, 'Oh.'

I reply with sadness in my eyes as I say, 'I know.'

Before the situation gets any worse – why would two women stop and start whispering on the street late in the evening – Petra says, ‘I don’t think he saw you. Let’s walk past them quickly.’

As we walk past them I keep my head down.

When we are in a safe distance, Petra says, ‘Maybe they broke up.’

I think about it, but then I remember that they still live together, so I reply, ‘They still live together. Would you keep living with someone you broke up with?’

Petra gives a very decisive, ‘No.’

‘Well, there you have it.’

Petra doesn’t want this incident to ruin the night, so she suggests, ‘Let’s forget about it and just dance the night away.’

Let me just say that I came home very late. Or very early, depends on how you look at it. And I think Petra turned off the alarm clock. At least, I hope she did.

Chapter 6

A week has passed since us reliving our student days and I must admit that the first few days were quite brutal – I don't know how we managed to spend the night out dancing and then go to classes fresh as a daisy the next day during. I must be getting old.

I reckon that some fresh air will do me good, so I decide to walk home from work. My sister Maya phones me and we have a nice, long chat. It's not the same as talking face-to-face, but at least we have this. As I am putting my phone into my purse, and looking down of course, I bump into someone. What can I say – I'm rather clumsy. I immediately start apologizing, but I am cut before I finish.

The person I bumped into says my name which surprises me as I don't know that many people here, so I look up with wide eyes and a slightly open mouth, and I notice David.

'Oh, hi, David! I'm sorry for ...' I manage to say when I notice he looks quite sad. 'You don't look so well. Is something wrong?'

'Rob moved out a couple of days ago and took Goldie with him.'

I can see that this has hit him quite hard, and I kind of regret asking the question, because I should have guessed it had something to do with Robert, but my brain is still half-asleep, I guess. I reply, 'Oh, no, that's sad.' I hate situations like these because I am not good at dealing with other people being sad. I want to help, but most of the time there's nothing really you can do.

David continues, 'Yeah. He got a job in Seattle and since Goldie is his dog, he took her with him.'

Hmm, so he doesn't know about Rob cheating on him. Or maybe it is just too painful for him to talk about, or maybe it's because this is very personal and we aren't really friends.

'I really feel for you,' I say. 'Is there anything I can do to make you feel better?' I know that in such situations nothing really helps … well, maybe ice cream can slightly ice the wounded heart, but in reality, time is the best healer. Time and falling in love again.

'I'll be fine, I just need to get used to it.'

'And in the mean time you have to do some fun things.' This is the advice Petra once offered me and it did the trick.

There's a silence for a few seconds and my mind starts panicking slightly because I don't know what to say. Then, an image of ice cream pops into my head, so I suggest, 'Listen, I was going to get some ice cream and just walk around town. Want to join me?'

That brings a smile on his face and he replies, 'Who could say no to ice cream?'

'The ultimate comfort food. They have a really great one a block from here.' The thought of ice cream gives me a bit more energy.

'I thought that someone who's into sports as much as you wouldn't eat ice cream.'

I laugh and reply, 'Oh, god no, I could never be one of those people, I love food too much.' This is the absolute truth. I think that my last meal would last a week because I would want to eat so much food – Szechuan chicken, lasagna, moussaka, banana crumble, peach crumble, blueberry muffins, bowls of salad, tortillas, fajitas, carob cake, apple strudel, baked pancakes with cottage cheese, cheesecakes, watermelons, and I could go on and on. But I only say, 'You just have to find a nice balance. If I did sport only to burn off calories, it would feel like a chore and I would start hating it. I do it because it makes me feel great.'

'I guess now that I have more time, I should get back to running. I used to love it in high school and college.'

I could tell he must have done some sports in his past because he looks quite fit. I don't say this to him, of course, I only say, 'Since the weather is always great in California, you can do it all year long. That's one of the reasons I moved here.'

'Oh, where are you from?'

'Colorado.'

'And you don't miss winter?'

I laugh out loud and reply, 'Not even for a second.'

He starts laughing as well. Maybe because it just shot out of me, I didn't even need a second or two to think about it.

I add, 'I don't ski or snowboard, so every October I would start counting down the days till spring.' A true fact. I dislike winter with a passion.

'Then California is perfect for you,' he adds.

My thoughts exactly!

After thinking about it for a few seconds, I add, 'I admit that the heat can be a bit too much at times, but there's always ice cream to cool you down.'

Speaking of ice cream, we arrive at the ice cream parlor and we enter. He is a true gentleman because he opens and holds the door for me. I'm glad some men still have good manners. Kudos to his parents!

I've been here several times. I like that they have a wide variety of ice creams and that they are home-made and made from fresh ingredients.

I already know which flavor I want, so I say, 'May I have stracciatella, please?'

David takes a bit longer and then decides on hazelnut. The shop assistant gives us the ice creams in cups, and I take my wallet out of the purse and pay. Because I don't want to deal with a bruised ego in case he finds this emasculating, I explain, 'It's on me because I invited you.' Besides, he doesn't have a wallet with him – I noticed this when he said he might start running again. Yes, I looked at his behind.

He replies, 'Then the next one is on me,' to which I agree.

When we get out of the parlor, he says, 'I've never met anyone who had stra…'

'Stracciatella,' I help him. 'It's a combination of vanilla ice cream and chocolate flakes, and it's pure heaven. Here, try some.'

He takes some with his spoon.

‘Wow, it really is good.’

‘But their hazelnut ice cream gets second place.’ I’m not just saying this to be polite. I’ve tried it and it is divine.

David tries his ice cream and says, ‘Next time, I should get half a scoop of each.’

‘Or just have two scoops,’ I suggest with a smile, and he smiles back. You see, I told you ice cream fixes a broken heart.

He agrees with me and says, ‘Good thinking.’

A man who cherishes a woman for her brain! He’s a keeper.

Seeing his mood improve, I quickly grab my chance and ask, ‘Besides ice cream, what else makes you smile?’

He thinks for a few seconds and then replies, ‘I love surfing. I love rollercoasters. Hanging out with friends.’ He looks at me when he says the last sentence. I guess he considers me a friend.

I’ve always had a soft spot for those in need, just ask all the stray cats that were fed by me, so it’s no surprise that I spend quite a lot of time with him in the next couple of weeks. I’ve always wanted to learn surfing, but I’ve just never come around to trying it. It might have something to do with my fear of sharks, but David reassured me that there are hardly ever any shark attacks in California, so he’s been showing me the ropes. I’m getting quite good at it – must be the fact that I used to train gymnastics so balancing on a surfboard is relatively easy compared to the balance beam.

We’ve also been on some rollercoaster rides. Those proved not to be a hit with me, at least after riding 5 of them in a row, so David had to enjoy the last three on his own. It was either that or him seeing what I had for lunch a few hours ago.

Playing table football is something I used to do a lot of – what else can you do in winter in Colorado when you don't ski or snowboard – but I did let David win a couple of times. After all, I was trying to make him feel better.

This evening we decided to go on a walk. It's a warm night and we've been walking for about an hour or so when I notice a playground with swings. There isn't anyone there, so I suggest we go there. Besides, it's nice to sit down after a long walk.

After a minute or two, David enthusiastically says, 'I haven't done this since I was a kid.'

'Don't tell anyone but I come here quite often.' Usually in the evening or early morning when there aren't any children here, because it wouldn't be nice to be swinging while a bunch of children are waiting their turn. 'It makes you feel like a kid again, doesn't it?'

'It does,' he says, still smiling. 'Back then life seemed so simple and fun. I mean, the only goal of the day was to have fun, just as much fun as possible.'

This makes me rest my head on the swing's chain and think about being on the swings as a child.

'Ah, the good old days,' I say with my mind taking me 20 years back.

David stops swinging, looks at me and says, 'I want to thank you,' with a serious tone in his voice.

The way he says it just sends a shiver down my spine. You can fell that he is being absolutely sincere. I stop swinging, look at him and ask, 'What for?'

'For making these past few weeks fun.'

I've never had someone thank me for such a thing, and I am deeply moved. I actually have to clear my throat before I reply, 'You're welcome. And I enjoyed them, too – everything's always more fun when you have someone to share it with.'

'True,' he says with a warm smile.

I want to lift the seriousness of this moment, so I ask, 'And you know what's also fun?'

He looks at with me with excitement in his eyes and asks, 'What?'

'Swinging high,' I reply with a broad grin. 'Terrifying and fun at the same time,' I add and start swinging high.

Seeing that he hasn't joined me, I try to encourage him by saying, 'Come on!' and it works.

I think we keep swinging for about 20 minutes or so, and then decide to go back home. After all, it is a school night.

As we enter the elevator, he surprises me with a compliment, saying, 'You're fun to be around.'

I instantly blush and look down. I'm not very good at receiving compliments. Maybe because I don't generally receive them.

Just as I am about to thank him, he says, 'I'm surprised you don't have a boyfriend.'

That completely catches me off guard and all I can manage to say is, 'Yeah, well.'

To rub a bit more salt to my wound he says, 'No, seriously.'

He, of course, doesn't do this on purpose because he doesn't know about my painful dating history. Without revealing too much, I only say, 'There's only so much heart break a girl can take.' I'm just not comfortable with sharing very personal information with others; I'd rather just suffer on my own.

I can hear that his mood also changes when he says, 'Yeah, heartbreaks suck. They can really bring you down.'

Neither of us wants to dampen our spirits, so we just wish each other good night and off to dreamland we go.

Chapter 7

A few days ago, Petra came into my classroom raving about the best book she has ever read and urging me to read it. She was talking about *5 Love Languages* and she was kind enough to lend me her copy. Since my love life has been non-existent in recent years, the title sparks my interest, so I decide to start reading it immediately. And let me tell you, the book is so good that I read it in one afternoon.

The author talks about how there are 5 languages of love, and that each person has a primary one. According to the author, people express love in five different ways: some express it by giving gifts, some by giving quality time, some by words of affirmation, some by acts of service (favors), and some by physical touch. Each person has one language of love that is primary – so if a person's primary language of love is physical touch, it means that this person needs physical touch from a loved one (parent, partner, or friend) to know that they love them.

It might be that your parents' language of love is giving gifts, but yours is words of affirmations, and because you perceive love as being love when someone offers words of affirmation, you believe that your parents don't love you because they don't praise you even if they show you love (according to them and their language of love) with buying you many gifts.

I am so inspired by the book that today I am prepared to share the knowledge with my pupils. I feel that it's very important that children and their parents learn about their languages of love so that they can start expressing love in the way that their child perceives it as love. This would make sure that children feel loved and this is basically what every child, no, make that every person, yearns for.

I distribute blank pieces of paper and when each has two, I start telling them about the task, 'Now, children, I want you to listen to my next question and just think about it. Don't give me an answer, just think about it, OK?'

The pupils nod, so I ask, 'How do you know that your parents love you?'

They are quiet, and some of them look slightly confused, so I offer further explanation, 'How do you know your mummy loves you? What does she do that makes you know she loves you?'

I pause for a second, just to let this sink in, and then I ask, 'How do you know your daddy loves you? What does he do that makes you know he loves you?'

The pupils start smiling, so I know they understand my questions.

'OK, now that you've had a chance to think about it, I want you to take the two pieces of paper I've given you.'

Children take the two pieces of paper. I also take two and hold them in front of me. I take a pen and demonstrate as I say, 'Now, I want you to write 'Mummy' on one piece of paper, and then 'Daddy' on the other piece.'

They write as instructed.

'Now take the paper with Mummy written on it and write down 'Mummy, I know you love me because' and then I want you to write down any ideas that come to your mind. When you are done with Mummy, do the same for Daddy.'

The pupils start thinking and writing. After some time I notice that one of them, James, isn't writing, so I go to his desk and ask him what the matter is.

'I don't know what to write for my dad. I don't know if he loves me.'

I try to help him and ask, 'Well, does he play with you? Or buy you presents?'

'He does.'

I see that he is still sad, so I know that these two activities don't resonate with him. I start the sentence for him with, 'But …' and James finishes it with, 'I would like him to hug me.'

I ask him, 'Does your mum hug and cuddle you?'

James's face lights up and he smiles and says, 'Oh, yes, every day.'

I am happy to hear that he receives love in the way he perceives as love from at least one parent. I suggest, 'OK, then how about you write a letter to your dad and tell him that you really like it when your mum hugs and cuddles you and that you would really like it if he did it as well?'

James nods and starts writing.

When they finish, I give them an envelope and tell them to put the letters into the envelope and give them to their parents when they come home. I've also typed a letter to the parents, explaining the task in detail because my pupils are a bit too young to be able to explain it properly on their own.

Chapter 8

A rainy day is perfect for relaxing at home, reading a good book and drinking some hot chocolate. Am I doing this right now? I wish! Instead, I am grading some tests – oh, joy!

Just as I get up to put the kettle on, I hear a knock at the door. I am not expecting anyone and it is a bit too late for the postman. I open the door and it's David. He's wearing a suit and tie, which is really unusual of him, but I must admit that he looks amazing. He should wear this more often.

I invite him in, but he says, 'I can't, I'm running to an audition. I just wanted to ask you if you have time tomorrow evening?'

'Sure, what's happening then?'

'A friend of mine is organizing Activity night and I could use someone smart in my team,' he says with a smile on his face.

I blush slightly and reply, 'Thanks for the compliment, but I should warn you that I am a terrible drawer.' I think the word terrible is even too mild to describe my drawing skills.

He laughs and says, 'You can't be worse than me.'

'I have my doubts, but I guess we'll see tomorrow.' Hopefully, it will be him doing the drawing.

He says goodbye and I wish him luck at the audition.

By next evening all the tests have been graded, so I can relax completely and enjoy the night. I was a bit worried about what his friends are like and if we'd hit it off, but they are a bunch of down-to-earth and fun people.

I've never played Activity before, but my sister Maya has. A group of couples would get together and play it every now and then, and Maya would tell me the next day how some of the couples got into arguments, all because of a game. I don't think her boyfriend and her got into any because she would always talk about others and we'd laugh. I think that later on, to avoid any potential break-ups, they decided to make teams of two people who weren't a couple.

We play it in Ian's apartment. David and I are one team, and then there are Ian and Howard, and Mark and Emma. What can I say about them? Well, Howard is tall and well-built and he's got blond hair and blue eyes. He is very funny and quite easy-going, and I'm guessing he's got lots of female admirers. He seems to be in his early 30s, while Ian seems more of David's age. Ian's got black hair and green eyes and is about the same height as David. He is also quite handsome and funny. Emma and Mark are both in their late 20s and they are boyfriend and girlfriend. You can see that they've been together for quite some time but they are still affectionate with each other.

We've been playing for about one hour now and we are just one task away from finding who the winner is.

Mark says, 'I don't think it's ever been so tense,' which just adds to the tension that is already in the room.

Emma adds, 'Yeah. Who would have thought David would ever have a chance of winning?'

David looks slightly offended when he hears it and says, 'Hey!' but then he starts smiling and adds, 'But you're absolutely right.'

David and Emma smile back. It's nice to have friends who you can be completely honest and open with, knowing that if you say something not nice (but truthful) it won't lead into an argument.

Ian makes the sound of the drumroll and says, 'The moment of truth.' He stands up and picks up a card.

Emma takes a mobile phone and sets the timer. She looks at Ian and asks him if he's ready. He nods, so she tells him to begin and she presses the start button on the timer.

All eyes are on him as he is showing his phrase with pantomime.

Howard looks unsure when he asks, 'Someone got killed?'

Ian nods, much to Howard's relief.

Howard continues guessing.

'And you are a detective? Sherlock?'

Ian shakes his head.

Howard goes on, 'Agatha Christie?'

Ian gives a surprised look and shakes his head. We are all laughing because the face he makes is absolutely priceless. Ian continues to show someone being killed and someone being happy about it.

Howard is still lost, but continues guessing and asks, 'How to kill a mocking bird?'

The buzzer goes off. Ian lets out a frustrated 'Argh!' and lifts his hands in despair as he says it.

'No, it was 'How to get away with murder'. How could you not get it?'

But clearly this doesn't affect Howard, because he seems quite chilled out and only says, 'Relax, man, it's only a game.'

Ian sits down next to David, still visibly being slightly upset.

David touches my knee with his hand and says, 'We're next.'

I don't know whether it's the nerves from being next or the fact that he has touched me, but in that second I become even more nervous. I slowly stand up, go to the blackboard, look at David and say, 'I apologize for my drawing in advance.'

I say a prayer, pick up a card and start thinking about how to draw my word. Ian takes the mobile phone and sets the timer. He looks at me, I nod, and he tells me to start drawing.

My hands are shaking, but I manage to draw a decent image of an archaeologist. His legs and arms are basically just straight lines, but I guess that is expected of someone who is terrible at drawing.

David tries to guess, but all his suggestions are wrong. When Ian says, 'Ten seconds!', David stands up and you can see that he is nervous. I draw an urn, and that is when he says the correct answer.

I am so happy that I lift my hands up and say, 'Yes!'

David starts jumping up and down, just like an excited and happy child would, and then he runs towards me, lifts me up and spins me around while saying, 'We've won!'

I don’t think I’ve ever seen him this happy. I guess this really means a lot to him. Judging by a box of my favorite chocolates that I find at my doorstep the next day also proves it.

Chapter 9

The days are getting shorter and you can feel it in the air that fall has come. It's Halloween tomorrow and I am in the kitchen baking some Halloween cookies for my pupils. I've already baked the first batch and have one tray in the oven, while the next one is already on the table, waiting its turn. The cookie cutters are lying scattered on the table and I grab the furthest one and make two cookies and put them onto the tray. The timer rings, so I take a tray out of the oven and put the cookies into the bowl. I take off the mitts, pick up the bowl, smell the cookies, and smile. Nothing beats the smell of freshly-baked cookies.

Just as I am enjoying the wonderful scent, the doorbell rings. I walk to the door and open it.

'Oh, hi, David. Come in.'

As he is coming in, he says, 'I was just walking past your apartment and something smelled so good.'

'I'm baking some cookies for my pupils for Halloween.'

I lead him into the kitchen. He looks at the tray on the table with cookies on it and says, 'Wow, these look amazing. I guess you really are a cookie lady.'

I smile, take the tray with cookies on it and put it into the oven. I don't lie when I say, 'These are pretty easy to make.'

'Let me see if they taste as good as they look,' he says and reaches for a cookie.

I gently slap him on his hand and say half seriously, 'Hey, they are for the pupils! Besides, they taste much better the next day.'

David still takes one cookie and bites into it.

'They already taste like heaven to me,' he says while munching on one. 'Can I take some home so I can test your theory then?' he asks with a naughty smile.

I cannot help but smile back. I reply, 'Well, if you are going to eat some, you should help me make more. I can't show up with three cookies tomorrow.'

'Sure. So, what do you want me to do?' he asks and looks around the table to see what he could do.

I sound like a teacher when I say, 'First, wash your hands.' I take an apron out of a drawer and tell him to put it on once he's washed his hands.

When he does as asked, I hand him a bowl and give him the instructions.

'Now, take this bowl and put 2 cups of flour, 2 cups of oats, 1 cup of chocolate chips, and 1 teaspoon of baking soda into it, and stir well.'

The only thing he says is 'OK', so I continue, 'And while you are doing that, I will do the other part. And then we will just mix the two together.'

'Sounds pretty simple,' he replies with confidence, so I am sure the process will be fun.

'It is.'

We spend the next minutes preparing the dough. When we are finished, I tell him to just start making cookies.

He looks around the table, thinks for a second and says, 'I'll take the bat one because you already have loads of ghost and pumpkin cookies.'

'Perfect. And I will do some witches.'

Now that the difficult part is behind us, I mean you do have to concentrate a bit while making the dough, we start talking. He asks me if I've always wanted to become a teacher.

'No. When I was younger, I wanted to be a gymnast.'

'And what happened?'

'My mum couldn't afford it.' She was a single parent, and practice and leotards cost money. I ask him about his dreams.

He smiles and replies, 'Well, first I wanted to be a policeman, then a pilot, and then in the 6th grade I caught the acting bug.'

'Wow, so early?' I don't think I've ever heard someone say they wanted to be an actor when they were still in elementary school. Mind you, this was when film stars weren't such big celebrities as nowadays when you see them everywhere – on magazines, on the Internet, in the news, etc. – and everyone wants to be like them because it means you will have lots of money and fans. Back then it was still more about the craftsmanship.

'We had this amazing teacher, Mrs. Owen. I guess she saw something in me and convinced me to try it for a year, and after the first performance I was hooked.'

‘That’s nice.’

He looks at me and with a serious tone he says, ‘So I have a deep respect for your profession. You can really influence and change people’s lives.’

‘So can *you*,’ I reply. ‘You can make people happy, sad, inspire them.’ Who hasn’t wanted to love more after seeing *Love Actually,* or do more good after seeing *Pay it Forward.*

‘I guess you’re right,’ he says.

‘Speaking of acting, how’s it been going?’ I’m genuinely interested in this because he never brings this topic up on his own. I think he’d even not talk about it if he got nominated for an Oscar.

‘I did some commercials in the past few weeks. And I am learning a script now.’

‘Anything interesting?’

‘A romantic comedy, so something you’d like,’ he says and accompanies it with a smile.

I, on the other hand, put on a serious face, put one hand on my hip, and say, ‘Why? Because I’m a woman and all women like them?’ I try to look really offended by his words and I try to keep the tone of my voice really sharp, but I am laughing on the inside.

I guess my performance deserves an Oscar because he immediately starts apologizing, ‘No, I mean …’

But before he can finish his apology, I start laughing. I’ve never really been good at lying or hiding my true emotions. I always laugh when I try to tell a lie, so pranking someone is almost impossible.

'I'm just joking. I love them,' I say when I manage to stop laughing. 'I'll keep my fingers crossed for you then.'

'Thanks,' he replies, visibly relieved that I was only joking. Then, he looks at all the cookies and says, 'We've made loads of cookies. How many pupils have you got? Because it looks like you could feed a school.'

'They aren't just for my pupils, some are also for Petra's, some for my co-workers, and then some for you and me.'

'Oh, good, because I have already started imagining us at the gym 24/7.'

Chapter 10

Speaking of gym, I must commend Petra for regularly coming to the gym with me. She does only come once a week, but that's one more visit per week than before. She even surprised me today when she asked me if we could meet up half an hour earlier. I guess she wants to burn off those cookies I brought her to school today.

While we are warming up, she asks, 'So, how's it going with that cute neighbor of yours?'

I am a bit puzzled by her question, so I ask, 'You mean David?' just to make sure we are talking about the same person. 'You do remember that I told you he is gay, right? So nothing like that is going on with him. We just hang out.'

'Quite often, may I add,' she says with a smile on her face.

It's true. We've been hanging out quite often in the past couple of months. I explain, 'I really enjoy his company. He is very smart, extremely funny, friendly, supportive, and he likes sports. What's also great is that I don't feel nervous around him like I would if he were straight. I can just be myself and it feels great.'

I don't think she's jealous that I spend so much time with him and not her, because she has recently started seeing a man named Richard, so she hasn't had that much time for us.

'Why do all great men have to be either in a relationship or gay?' she asks and gives a sigh.

'Tell me about it!' I commiserate with her.

'Has he got any cute friends?'

Here she goes again with trying to find me a boyfriend. I tell her that I am not really looking for a relationship but then she surprises me with saying, 'Hey, I am asking for me.'

'What happened to Richard?' I thought things were going fine.

'It turns out he still isn't over his ex,' she replies and adds an eye roll.

'I hate it when that happens. But at least he figured it out at the beginning of your relationship.'

'But I'm still slightly bummed,' she says and I give her a hug.

'You've been really good at going to the gym regularly, and who knows, maybe you will meet someone nice here. Someone who *is* single and available.'

'Hey, that goes for you, too.'

I'm glad she doesn't suggest speed dating again.

She puts extra effort today and does more repetitions than ever before – we even try boxing! Doing sports is perfect for letting off steam, I'm telling you.

I suggest we meet up later in the day, but she can't because they're celebrating her mum's birthday. We say goodbye and I can't wait to get home and have a shower. I'm drenched in sweat.

After the shower, I just catch up on the news when there's a knock at the door. It's David. It looks like he didn't have a good night's sleep because he's got slightly visible bags under the eyes but he's still quite cheerful. After saying hello, he asks me if I have a few minutes to spare. As I am not doing anything important, I say, ‘Sure, what’s up?’

‘I’ve got an audition in a couple of days and I was wondering if you could help me run the lines.’

So that’s why he’s not been sleeping, he’s probably been memorizing the lines. I’ve always wanted to see how actors prepare, so I don’t hesitate and reply, ‘Sure. Do you want to do it here or shall we go to your place?’

‘My place. I left the script there.’

I take the keys, lock my apartment and we go to his place. We sit down on the sofa and he gives me the script.

‘Just so you know, I’ve never done this,’ I say. ‘I don’t know whether I should also get into the character or just read out the lines without conveying any emotions.’

‘It doesn’t matter. Whatever suits you best. I just need someone to practice the dialogue with.’

Just as we are about to start, his phone rings.

‘Go ahead,’ I say and motion with my hand and head that he should answer it. ‘And while you are talking, I will just quickly read through the script.’

David goes and answers the phone, and I read a few pages. This will help me get to know what’s going on so I can use proper tone when reading my lines.

When he returns, he asks if I am ready.

'Yup. And please don't laugh at my acting.' I've decided to try and act it out because I think this will help him say his lines more convincingly.

The scene is about a couple having a fight and they are yelling at each other. The first time I have to yell at him I start apologizing afterwards – I guess this just shows that I wouldn't be that good of an actress – but he just encourages me to give it my all. We are standing up as we are reading the lines because I think that's more probable. I don't know if I've ever had a real fight while sitting down.

Anyway, the male character has been spending a lot of time with a friend, who's a woman, and his girlfriend doesn't like that, she thinks he is cheating on her. It turns out that she's been helping him teach him how to dance because he wants to impress her at their upcoming wedding. You can tell that I am uncomfortable when he is apologizing to my character and is holding my hand and is telling my character why he loves her, because I start laughing, but I put my script in front of my face so that me laughing doesn't distract him. Then, he stops talking and takes a step closer. I guess it's my character's turn to say something, so I look at the script and see that it says we kiss. I gasp, look at him, nervously take my hand out of his, and just say that we can leave the last part out.

He replies, 'Oh, yeah, we usually also leave it out during auditions.'

After a moment of silence, I say, 'I really don't know how you actors do it.'

He doesn't quite understand what I mean because he asks, 'Do what?'

'Get so physically intimate with another person that you don't know or love. Or maybe it's just me.'

'What do you mean?' he asks with a puzzled look on his face.

Damn, why did I have to open my mouth? But there's no way of going back, so I say, 'I just get really uncomfortable when people touch me.'

He thinks for a second, then says, 'But I've seen you touch people.'

'Oh, I don't have a problem with touching people. I often do it without thinking about it, it just comes naturally. But I do have a problem when other people touch *me*.'

'I hadn't noticed that.'

'Because I usually don't say anything, I just slowly move my hand or my leg a bit or make a gesture that ends the physical touch.'

Most people don't notice that them touching me makes me uncomfortable, because I don't think it shows on my face, and I also move away from them very subtly. I guess if someone else was observing me and the person touching me, they would notice it, but the person touching me mostly doesn't.

David is in a pensive mood for a few seconds and then asks, 'Does it make you uncomfortable when I touch you?'

'Damn, now I wish I hadn't mentioned it.'

'So it does.' He looks sad when he says it.

I try my best to comfort him. ‘Not always,’ I quickly add. ‘And it doesn’t mean that I don’t like you or anything like that, really, I swear.’

He still looks sad. I hate seeing him like this. I don’t know how to make it go away, but I try with explaining the situation a bit more.

‘It’s a general thing, although I must admit that it happens more when it comes to men than women.’

He is very careful when he asks, ‘Did something happen to you that started it?’

I see what he is implying, so I calm him.

‘Well, I wasn’t sexually abused by a man if that’s what you are thinking.’

‘Thank god,’ he says, visibly relieved.

‘I’ve given it quite a thought actually. I guess there are two reasons that come to my mind – one is that my mum and dad split when I was six and I didn’t really have much contact with him, so I am not used to getting affection from men and I don’t know how to interpret it when I get some. Is it just a friendly gesture or do they want more? I lived with my mum and she never embraced or hugged me when I was younger. She wasn’t a particularly warm person, so I guess my body is just not used to being touched.’

‘I’m sorry to hear that.’

‘It’s not your fault, so your apology is not necessary.’

‘And what’s the other thing?’ he asks carefully.

'Hmm, probably the fact that she was physically abusive, so physical touches meant something bad, painful, something that you wouldn't really want.'

'Wow, I don't know what to say.' He looks shocked. 'But now I get it.'

'Get what?' I ask.

'Why you're afraid to love. I mean, the two people who were supposed to give you unconditional love failed you and hurt you.'

He is a man of wise words. It's why I'm afraid to open up to people, because my trust has been betrayed so many times, and when I do open up, I often end up getting hurt.

I say, 'Yeah, and then when someone else hurts you, it just breaks your heart that's already in pieces even more.' And right now, I feel my heart has been broken too many times, so I've become emotionally unavailable.

There's a moment of silence.

'I would hug you but you've just said you don't like it,' he says with a sad look in his eyes.

I smile at him, trying to convey that I am thankful just for the nice thought. I don't think I could handle a hug right now – telling him about something so personal has left me feeling quite exposed, vulnerable, and emotional, and I cannot deal with a physical touch when I am in such a state. I might break down and cry.

I try to lighten the mood and say, 'Enough about me. I came here to help *you*, so let's do the scene again. Let me just get into my actor zone.' I accompany the last sentence with a hand gesture that suggests I am trying to get centered and into the zone – it looks a bit funny, so it's just the right thing to get past the seriousness of the conversation we've just had.

Chapter 11

I had a really good day at work today. Correct that – I had an amazing day! James, the pupil who wanted his father to hug him more, stayed in the classroom after the last lesson, came up to me and thanked me for the letter writing activity that we did a couple of weeks ago. He told me that his father now hugs him in the morning before he goes to work, when he comes from work, and before bedtime. You could see the happiness in James's face and I have also noticed that he has been more peaceful lately and that he's been smiling more often. When I asked him how he feels now, he gave the most amazing answer, 'Like my heart has been healed.'

Ah, bless his little soul. It's really nice when you can make a difference in someone's life. I told Petra about it and she is going to give it a try with her class tomorrow.

I am beaming with pride and my heart is full of love and joy as I am walking home from work. It's just one of those moments when everything seems right, like everything is just the way it is supposed to be. Suddenly, I hear a man's voice say, 'Someone's in a good mood!' and I look into the direction it came from. I'm surprised to see it is David who said it.

'Oh, hi! I didn't see you there. I just had a really nice day at work.'

'That's nice to hear,' he replies. 'Do you want to go for walk?'

'Sure.'

We walk a bit and then we sit down on a bench. After some time, he says, 'Hey, Tina, I've been thinking about what you said the other day.'

'I say so many amazing things every day.' As you can see, I am still drunk on that outpour of gratitude from an hour ago. We both smile, and ten I add, 'You'll have to be more specific.'

'About how you don't like it when people touch you.'

No, no, no, don't kill my great mood. In a sad voice I say, 'Oh, that thing.'

He immediately apologizes, 'Oh, sorry, I didn't mean to make you sad.'

'No, it's fine,' I lie a bit, 'you just caught me a bit off guard.'

He seems excited when he says, 'So, I've been thinking. This is a problem for you and you wish you didn't feel like that anymore, right?'

'Yeah, that would be nice,' I say hesitantly. What is he on about?

'You said that when other people touch you, you feel uncomfortable because you are not used to it. So, I was thinking that maybe your cure would be to get physical with other people every day so that your body would get used to this.'

I think about his words for a moment. 'That's an interesting suggestion. The only problem is that I can't just go running around, telling people to touch my hand or hug me. It would be a bit strange.'

He victoriously says, 'That's why I have come up with a plan.'

'Uh, a plan?' I ask skeptically. This is so typical of men – when they encounter a problem, they must solve it, whereas we women talk about our problems just to get the frustration out of our system, not always wanting the person listening to us to come up with a solution. Sometimes talking about it is the solution.

'You can say 'No' to it, but I think it would really help you.'

I am intrigued, so I say, 'Let's hear it then.'

He takes a deep breath and says, 'OK, so I was thinking that I could help you, I mean I could be the one that you would practice on.'

'What do you mean by practice?' I ask and give him a questioning look.

'Well, we could start slowly, let's say we would hold pinkies for a few minutes several times a day.'

I start imagining this scene in my mind. We're at home, watching a movie and holding pinkies. It does raise my anxiety levels a bit, but it isn't something I couldn't handle, so I say, 'OK.'

He explains his plan further and says, 'And when you feel comfortable with that, we would move on to, let's say, holding hands.'

As he is saying these words, I'm already picturing it in my mind, and I tremble.

'Ah, just the thought of this makes me nervous.'

'As I said, you can say no.'

The way he says it shows that he really wouldn't be offended if I decide not to do it.

'No, I mean, I can see why you thought of that. It's like when someone is terrified of spiders, and then they are made to touch and hold a spider in their hands until they get comfortable doing so, and their phobia lessens or disappears.' This reminds me – I shouldn't tell him I am afraid of big, hairy spiders and heights. I don't want him to come up with crazy ideas, like bungee jumping for example. One issue at a time is all I can handle.

'Yeah, I thought that this could help you.'

I think about it for a few seconds and then say, 'OK, I will do it, but on one condition.'

'Name it.'

'That we do it slowly, that we don't rush it. I need to feel comfortable, and I usually don't feel comfortable when someone is rushing me or if circumstances demand me to rush. And that the moment it gets too much for me, we stop it. I don't mean that we stop the whole plan, but that we stop with that activity for that day.'

'Sounds OK to me.'

I'm glad he's OK with my conditions, but I still suggest, 'Let's shake on it.'

After we shake hands, I smile and say, 'I think I need a day or two just to mentally prepare for this.'

Chapter 12

I am a woman of my words, so when I've had a few days to prepare myself for David's plan, I go over to his apartment, and as soon as he opens the door, I say, 'OK, I am ready. Let's start the healing.'

He invites me in and asks, 'What should we do?'

'We can start with the pinky, like you suggested.'

He asks, 'So, do you want to do it standing up or would you prefer to sit down?'

'Hmm, let's sit down.' This might be better in case I faint. Besides, it would look really silly if we were standing in an apartment and holding pinkies.

We sit down and he wraps his pinky around mine. Instantly, I can feel heat rising in me. I don't know whether it's just because of this exercise, or because it is him that is touching me. My heart starts racing and it kind of feels like I am about to have a heart attack. I try to distract myself by imagining someone else holding my finger, and without even realizing I start humming a melody. David notices it and says, 'You're nervous.'

'What gave me away?' I hope I am not as red as a lobster.

He tries to calm me down and says, 'Just take a deep breath.'

I breathe in deeply.

'Hold it.'

He is looking at me, and by looking at me, I mean that he is looking at me with his gorgeous brown eyes. I can feel myself blushing. If he notices it and says something about it, I'm sure I can pass it as a consequence of holding my breath for so long.

He tells me to exhale, which I do.

'Better now?' he asks, and I nod.

We keep holding our pinkies for about a minute or more, and then I let go and explain, 'Sorry, this is as much as I can handle at this moment.' I exhale nervously as I say it. I continue, 'And it has nothing to do with you. In fact, I think that I would have let go much sooner if it were someone else.'

The way I see it is that because he is gay, he doesn't have an ulterior motive for doing this, he is simply doing it because he really wants to help me. This makes me feel safe, knowing that this pinky holding won't lead to him throwing himself on me, so I don't have to be nervous with anticipation of what is to come next like I would be if there was another man in his place. It's just pinky holding and that's it.

'That's nice to hear,' he says with a smile. 'So, how did you feel throughout the process?'

I tell him all about it in detail.

'After a few seconds, I could feel heat rising up in my body, and then it felt like my whole body was about to explode from so much heat, and that is when it became too much for me and I had to let go. And when I let go, my body started cooling down.'

'So it is like being in a sauna, and just as you feel like you are about to pass out, you get out.'

I can't help but laugh at his comparison. 'I guess you could say so. You know what, let's do it again.'

He gives me a surprised look.

'I know, even I'm surprised,' I tell him. 'I think that talking about it relaxed me.'

He offers me his pinky and I wrap mine around it.

After about a minute, I ask him, 'What if we talk while we are doing this? I won't be focused that much on it then.'

Luckily, he agrees and asks me what I'd like to talk about.

'Just anything,' I reply. Mindless chit-chat seems perfect, so I say, 'Let's start with how your day was.'

David starts talking about his day. After a while, we sit even more comfortably on the sofa, and I am only reminded that we are holding pinkies when one of us unintentionally breaks the hold when we want to accompany what we are saying with a hand gesture.

We do the same the next day, and then on the third day David suggests we start holding hands, or Phase 2 as he calls it. I am a bit apprehensive at first, mainly because this seems like it's not just one step away from holding pinkies, but ten. It's the real deal. With pinkies, only a smart part of my body was being touched, but when you hold hands, it's the whole hand! And what if my hand gets sweaty?

As it was the case with pinkies, we start holding hands just for a few seconds, and then add a bit more time each time. I barely make it through the first day. I have to make myself a nice, relaxing bath and put on some meditation music to calm down otherwise my mind would be analyzing the events all night long. The next few days are slightly easier, but I am taken aback at the weekend when he suggests we go hiking and then wants to hold my hand during the hike.

'But what if someone sees us?' I protest.

He thinks he's witty when he replies, 'Well, there are people on this hiking trail, so we will be seen.'

'Ha, ha,' I say and then I get to the gist of the problem. 'I mean, what is someone we know sees us?'

'Well, we can say that you are tired and I am helping you get to the top,' he replies after thinking for a few seconds. 'Or better yet, that you are helping *me* to the top. That sounds more believable.'

I don't know about you, but holding hands while hiking, especially if the hill is rather steep, is just extremely difficult. I've probably burnt 400 extra calories, so when we get down I invite him for lunch. I need to replenish my energy stores.

'Only if I can shower first,' he replies.

'Yeah, I think I need one, too,' I add. Burning extra 400 calories comes at a price.

He knocks on my door about half an hour later. He is wearing jeans, a top and a sweater, and I can smell that he's also added a splash of cologne. I normally don't like men's cologne because they all have a very strong scent, but the one he uses kind of reminds me of baby powder. It has a pleasant, fresh, cotton-like aroma and I could smell it all day and just get lost in it.

He produces a beautiful white rose from behind his back. I am very surprised and want to ask him when he had the time to get it, but he speaks before I can open my mouth and says, 'A beautiful rose for a beautiful lady.'

I smile and thank him, go into the kitchen, put it in a vase and place it on the dining table. Receiving gifts isn't my language of love, but it's nice to know that he took the time and went and bought it.

When we exit the apartment building, he gently takes my hand into his and then slowly runs his thumb along the back of my hand, which sends shivers down my spine and I get goosebumps. He holds my hand all the way to the restaurant, and on our way back he intertwines his fingers with mine. It feels strange at first, because I barely just got used to the previous hand holding; this new one seems even more intimate and sweaty. Is it always like this?

He remembers he needs some new trousers and asks me to come with him and help him choose. I didn't think he's someone who needs help with choosing clothes, because he just looks great no matter what he has on and the clothes he has all look great, so he clearly knows what to pick. I've never been clothes shopping with a man and I wonder if it's true that they are done in a matter of minutes.

About half an hour later I know that he doesn't belong into that category. I think he tries on about ten pairs and with every pair he asks 'Do I look professional in these?, Do they go well with this shirt?, Are the pockets too big?, Are the pockets too small?, Are the pockets on the back side too high?, Are they too low?'

I don't think I've ever stared at a man's behind for so long as I just have. Don't get me wrong - I'm not saying that this is a bad thing. The man's got a great butt, kind of on the smallish side, but it's perfect for his body type. And you can tell that he takes care of his body because it's firm.

OK, enough about his body parts, let's fast forward to a couple days later. I am sitting at home and watching TV when I get a text message from David. He asks me if I am busy, so I reply 'No. What's up?'

He texts back, writing 'Put on a dress and come to my place in 15 minutes. It's time for phase 3.'

Phase 3? What's phase 3? And why do I need a dress for it? I go into my bedroom, open the wardrobe and try to decide what dress to pick. Should I go for a short sleeved one or will long sleeves be better? I'm guessing we'll be somewhere inside because if we were outside, it would be too cold to have only a dress on and if I wore a coat over it, no one would even see that I was wearing a dress, so why would he tell me to wear one? Short sleeves it is. I decide to put on a purple one with a nice patter. I comb my hair, put all the essentials into my purse and I go to his apartment. I knock and I hear his voice say, 'It's open.', so I enter.

I cannot see him, so I ask relatively loudly, 'I'm afraid to ask but how many phases are there?'

'I don't know. I just play it by ear,' I hear him answer, and a few seconds he comes out of his bathroom. He is dressed nicely.

I blurt out, 'Wow, you look nice.'

He smiles and says, 'Thanks. And look at you!'

I blush gently. Because patience has never been a virtue of mine, I ask, 'So, where are we going? What are we doing?

He replies calmly, 'I've signed us up for dancing lessons.'

I start laughing nervously. My voice is shaking slightly when I say, 'Oh, God, you don't know what you got yourself into. I have two left feet.' And not to mention my fear of intimacy, and you have to be really close when you are dancing. I am fine when I am dancing on my own or with a few girlfriends but that's because it's just different with women.

He tries to calm me and says, 'Ah, you can't be worse than me.'

'Wait and see.' I don't think he's prepared for what he is about to experience. I just freeze and become stiff. People always assume that it's the men who have two left feet, but women can have them, too.

'Shall we go?'

I'm glad I've put on a dress with short sleeves because after an hour, I am sweating. Not much, but enough to want to jump into the shower.

A friend of his is the dance teacher and he is really patient with me. And David. I'm glad David isn't an expert at this because it would make me even more nervous. You can tell he has had some dance lessons before, because he can move, but we are almost at the same level.

And this dancing isn't as terrible as I thought it would be. I like it that there are steps you have to learn and then dance accordingly because it makes me feel more at ease if I know what's coming up next.

We go there twice a week – first, we learn the cha cha. It's a fun dance and perfect for me because there's little physical contact and also little eye contact because we are looking down at our feet most of the time, trying not to mess up and step on each other's feet. By next lesson, we've somewhat mastered it.

The waltz is the dance of the second, and our last, week. I've always loved this dance, because it looks simple, yet so beautifully romantic. First, we learn the basic steps without a partner. When we look confident enough, the teacher tells us to pair up. He then instructs the men to put their right hands on women's shoulder blades, and tells us ladies to put our left hands on our partner's right arm. David pulls me closer and I can feel my heartbeat become faster. We put our free hands together in a clasp. I can hear the teacher tell me to look up, which I do. When my eyes meet David's, I cannot help but blush and smile. It seems David is also nervous because he smiles back and then nervously looks down. The music starts and even though we were doing really well when we were dancing the waltz steps on our own, we have a hard time following the rhythm. It isn't because we are dance challenged, nerves just get the better of us. The teacher comes over and counts the steps as we dance, which is of great help. By the end of this lesson we manage not to step on each other's feet or hit each other with our knees once in a single dance. The next time is far more enjoyable, maybe because we also practiced at home. I can see why they say that dancing brings people closer together, not just physically but emotionally as well, and I am not surprised that so many dancing partners are also romantically involved. There's just something about being so close to your partner for at least one hour a day that makes you feel connected to them, even if you don't speak a word during the whole time. Maybe it's the music that sets the mood, or perhaps it's the emotions you are trying to convey with a dance, perhaps even that you are having fun together.

David has to work out of town the next few days, so the first time I hear from him is on Wednesday when I come home and find a note attached on my door and 'Phase 4 today at 7' written on it.

There's a phase 4? What's more intimate than dancing? I know that he wouldn't cross the line, but I still nervously wait for the clock to strike seven. I go over to David's and I become slightly suspicious when I see that he has some candles placed on the coffee table and shelves.

Before I get a chance to comment, he says, 'I thought we'd start with hugging today.'

I let out an unconvincing, 'OK,' and add, 'And why would we need candles?'

'Well, I was thinking. You always overthink everything and I thought that if we put some slow music on, turn the lights off, light some candles …'

I interrupt him and ask, 'Isn't this just a bit too romantic?' I don't say anything about his comment that I overthink everything, because a) it's completely true, and b) the candles are all I can focus on right now.

He replies, 'In a way, but I thought you'd feel more comfortable if it's dark, and if you put your favorite music on, you will be listening to it and singing along, so you won't analyze the hug. The candles are there just so that it isn't pitch dark.'

I think about it for a few seconds.

‘Hmm, you might be right.’

He looks pleased, points to his tablet and says, ‘Go and pick your favorite music and I’ll light the candles.’

‘And what if my favorite song is something really upbeat?’

David looks at me as if he is analyzing me.

‘Nah, it isn’t,’ he says. ‘You’re a romantic soul.’

‘You know me too well.’

I take his tablet and start searching Youtube videos. David moves the coffee table in the living room so we will have more space, then lights the candles. When he’s done, he asks me if I’ve already picked something.

I have a favorite song, but it’s way too romantic for two friends to be listening to while hugging, so I say, ‘No. This is hard.’

‘Let me help. The 6th song from the top.’

That’s a nice tactic. I count the songs and when I see it’s Ed Sheeran’s *Thinking Out Loud*, I say, ‘It might be a bit too romantic.’

He simply says, ‘It’s fine by me.’ He walks towards the light switch and turns the lights off.

He comes towards me. I press play. I don’t know what to do next, so I ask, ‘So, how do we do this?’ I mean, he came up with the plan, so he must have thought about how to go about it.

He takes another step towards me so that we are almost touching. I can feel his breath on my face and it makes me start breathing deeper and faster. He gently takes my arms and carefully puts them around his neck. He slowly traces his hands down my back, lets them rest on my waist and then gently pulls me in for a hug.

The music is playing and although I set the volume to a level that I could hear the lyrics and sing along to distract me from the hug, I cannot hear the words. All I can feel is David's hands on my waist, occasionally going up and down my back, and I can smell his cologne – the same cologne he had on when we went for lunch after the hike, the one that smells divine, the one that makes me just want to pull him even closer and hold him really tight and never let him go.

And then it happens. I start crying.

David doesn't let me go, but pulls me closer, gently caresses my back and says, 'Just let it out.'

It makes me cry even more. When I compose myself a bit, I pull out of the embrace and I say, 'I don't know what came over me. It just felt so good to be hugged and then something inside me just broke and tears started.'

He wipes away a tear from my left eye and I look down. I am slightly embarrassed by this mini breakdown. He kisses my forehead and then lifts my arms and puts them around his neck again. He puts his hands on my lower back and hugs me.

I don't know how long we stand there hugging, but it's long enough for my legs to start hurting. We do the same the next two evenings and what surprises me is that I actually look forward to it. It just feels so good.

On Saturday we decide to go to a concert. It's a nice change in mood from the previous days because we dance and sing and just have fun. I don't even find it that nerve-racking when a slow song comes on and he moves behind my back and wraps his arms around my waist. I blame it on the two beers he had. And the five sips I had. I was thirsty and I had drunk all my water.

I have to confess something. I find him attractive. Very attractive. Actually, I think I am in love with him. Completely. Madly. With every fiber of my being.

These past few weeks have been torture and heaven at the same time. Heaven because I've been able to enjoy his touches, him holding my hand, him giving me endless number of hugs, and just doing things that couples normally do. Heaven because now I know that I can be affectionate and accept affection from a man. Heaven because physical contact now feels pleasant and I want more of it. But the torture has also been great – knowing that this is just a dream, that this will never happen in real life with him, knowing that when he holds me, he feels nothing but friendship towards me. I worry about how I will be able to cope once the healing process is over. Will it crush me? Will it make me open up and look for love where it can be reciprocated? I guess only time will tell.

Chapter 13

I don't know how I feel about Christmas and New Year. On one hand I love the idea of family getting together, having a nice meal, exchanging gifts, celebrating starting a new year with a clean slate, but on the other hand it can be quite stressful. You see people driving like mad, the road rage is especially common, shops are full of people rushing and arguing, and it seems that the magic of Christmas is lost. That is why I prefer buying presents throughout the year – whenever I see something that I think a friend or family member would like, I buy it. Of course, you need some place to store the purchased items, but come December you have lots of wonderful things just waiting to be wrapped.

Speaking of wrapping presents, I have just found the most wonderful wrapping paper! It's silver with small green and silver circles, and it shimmers! It was love at first site, I'm telling you. And then I also found the same one but with pink and silver circles! It doesn't take much to make me happy.

A letter without a stamp on it is waiting for me in my mailbox. Curiosity gets the best of me, even thought my hands are full, and I immediately open it. In it there's a white paper with 'Be ready at 6. Dress warmly but comfortably.' I recognize David's handwriting. I wonder what he has planned this time. I like being spontaneous, but I have to admit that these kind of surprises make me slightly nervous. I check the time and see that I only have an hour left, so I rush home, have a shower, and get dressed.

The doorbell rings at 6 sharp. I love it when people are punctual, but that's teachers for you, I guess. I open the door and David is holding a blindfold in front of my face.

‘Put this on,’ is the only thing he says.

I lock the door, put on the blindfold, and take his hand.

A few minutes later we are sitting in a taxi.

‘Why won’t you tell me where you’re taking me?’ I ask.

‘Because it’s a surprise.’

‘I hate surprises. For all I know, you could be taking me into a dark forest where you will make me dig my own grave,’ I say with a serious face. If I didn’t have the blindfold on, he would also see my eyes widen as if I were really frightened.

He laughs and says, ‘I think you watch too many criminal series. Don’t worry, you’ll love it.’

I want to say something back, but the taxi stops and David gets out of it. I try to open the door but it’s a bit hard to do when you are blindfolded. Luckily, David opens the door, takes my hand, and helps me get out. He even puts his other hand on my head so that I don’t hit my head when I am getting out.

I wrap my arm around his, and we walk for a bit. I am trying to search for clues that would tell me where we are, but all I can hear is people talking and laughing and music playing, so if he plans on killing me, at least there’ll be witnesses.

‘We’re here.’

‘May I take the blindfold off?’

‘Yes.’

I slowly take it off, unsure of what to expect. And then I see an ice skating rink.

'Oh my God! I love it,' I say and start jumping up and down from joy. 'How did you know?'

'You told me how much you loved ice skating when you were younger, so I thought this would be a nice surprise.'

I think I mentioned this to him once while we were talking about something else, so I am extremely surprised that he remembered.

'What are you waiting for?' I say excited. 'Let's go!'

As we are putting on the ice skates, David says, 'I have to warn you that I've never done this.'

'Really? Never?' I ask surprised. Why would he bring someone here then as a surprise if he doesn't know how to ice skate? And then I use my reassuring voice, 'But don't worry, you'll get it in no time. It's very similar to rollerblading. You just need a few practice laps and then you'll be skating like a pro.'

We enter the rink, and he immediately grabs hold of the rail.

'This feels so strange,' he says with a scared face, 'and dangerous.'

I must admit that it is quite a strange feeling standing on ice skates after so many years. I thought it would be a piece of cake because I rollerblade quite often, but it definitely feels different.

'Take my hand,' I say and offer him my hand. 'We'll go really slow, OK?'

He looks a bit unsure whether he should do this, but he takes my hand and we start ice-skating. He's a bit wobbly, so he holds onto my hand tightly. We almost complete a lap when a child goes past him and throws him off balance, so he falls and takes me with him. That's what you get when you hold hands.

I start laughing really hard. I know I shouldn't but it looked so funny. He, on the other hand, has a painful expression on his face.

'This will leave a bruise.'

I'm still laughing when I reply, 'More than one. But isn't it fun?'

'A bit.' He manages a smile. 'How do I get up?'

'Really slowly.' I get off him and help him get back onto his feet.

'I think I owe you dinner after this,' he says when he is finally standing.

After that, ice skating is a breeze. He gets more confident with each lap and after an hour he is skating like a pro. Well, sort of.

My stomach begins growling – no wonder, the last time I had anything to eat was during school lunch break and that was hours ago.

'I think I need to eat something or I will turn into a monster,' I say with a smile.

'Perfect! Because I'm hungry, too. And my legs are starting to hurt.'

We head for a restaurant nearby. We've never been here and since there are quite a lot of people in it, it must be good. The waiter shows us to our table and brings us our drinks.

'I'm starving,' David says as he takes the menu and browses through it.

'Me too. Sport sure works up an appetite.'

After looking at the menu for a bit, he says, 'I think I'm in the mood for some pasta.'

Pasta sounds nice but I am in a mood for trying something new. 'I see they have seafood risotto. I've always wanted to try that.'

He raises his glass and says, 'Let's make a toast. To a wonderful evening!'

'To a wonderful evening! And to more ice skating!'

The waiter returns, ready to take our order. 'Have you decided?'

'Yes. May I have the seafood risotto?'

'And I'd like vegetable pasta, please.'

The waiter goes away, and I hope he brings our food sooner rather than later. I start picturing myself eating when David says, 'Listen, Christmas is a few weeks away. My parents are going on a cruise, so I am staying here, and I was thinking of having some friends over, have dinner, maybe go out for some drinks.'

'That sounds lovely.'

'Can you come or do you already have plans?'

'I'd love to come,' I reply. I don't have any plans for Christmas because I am flying over to my sisters' after Christmas. This way they can spend the holiday with their partner's or husband's families, and then we can have a relaxing get together afterwards.

‘I can bring some desserts,’ I offer. I mean, if I get invited to a Christmas get-together, at least I can do is bring some food.

‘Hmm, those rum balls you made a few weeks ago were amazing.’

I agree with him, they really were. I’m not really a fan of alcohol because most of it smells weird to me and I can’t have something that smells weird, but somehow rum has this pleasant aroma that I could just smell all day long. Smell, not drink, mind you.

My mind starts thinking of nice desserts, so I continue, ‘I can also bake some gingerbread cookies. And a banana cake roll – I made one with my pupils yesterday and it was a hit.’ In fact, it was such a hit, that we had to make another one so they could take some home for their parents.

‘Can’t wait to try it.’

‘Do you also need some help with the main dishes?’ I offer, but I am not that good with main dishes as I am with desserts.

‘I think we have that covered. I am making mashed potatoes and roasted vegetables, Mark is bringing his famous vegetable risotto, Emma mentioned mushroom soup and sauce, Howard is in charge of the turkey, and Ian is taking care of drinks.’

‘All this talk has made me even hungrier.’

Luckily, the food comes a few minutes later and it looks delicious. I am slightly disappointed by the taste of my seafood risotto, it seems it’s missing something, but I am so hungry I eat it anyway.

We walk home afterward and he is holding my hand the whole time. We also hug as we say goodnight and he even gives me a kiss on the cheek.

About an hour or so later, just as I am getting ready to go to bed, I start feeling heartburn. I guess I must have eaten too fast, so I take a Pepto-Bismol.

However, about an hour later the pain is still there, and when I turn to one side in my bed, it just seems to make the nausea worse. I start getting hot flashes and cold sweats and a terrible feeling in my stomach. I know what this leads to, so I rush to the bathroom where I am reacquainted with everything I ate today.

I must admit that I hate throwing up! I hate it so much that sometimes I'm on the verge of tears or I actually start crying *before* I even throw up, just because I know how awful it feels.

The nausea lessens slightly, so I go back to bed, but the toilet calls my name 4 or 5 more times in the next three hours or so. I can't really say the exact number because the vomiting is so severe that it just messes with my cognitive functions. I only remember that after the last visit to the bathroom, I am on the verge of tears but I can't shed a single one because I am so exhausted. I lie down and I am still in pain, so I know there is still some of what's causing me to be ill left in me, but I just can't move. While I would love to get rid of what's causing this, I just don't have the strength, I just can't take another visit to the bathroom. I'm praying that the pain will just stop and, luckily, after about twenty minutes I fall asleep.

A doorbell wakes me up a few hours later. I muster up all my energy to get up and open the door. I don't even bother putting on my morning robe.

It's David. He can see that I am unwell and asks with a worrisome face, 'Oh, no, what's wrong?'

He enters the apartment, gently takes my hand, and leads me to the sofa in the living room.

'I think the seafood didn't agree with me. I was in the bathroom the whole night.' I don't go too much into details because people in generally don't want to hear about disgusting things.

'How can I help? Shall I make you some peppermint tea?'

'That would be great, thanks.' I lie down on the sofa, cover myself with the blanket, and David goes into the kitchen to make the tea. He comes back with a cup in his hands.

'Here's some tea.'

By then I am already in the land of dreams, so he puts the tea on the coffee table in front of the sofa.

The next thing I hear is a door being shut, and I open my eyes to see David at the door with a grocery bag in his hands.

He looks at me and sees that I've woken up. 'Oh, I didn't want to wake you up,' he says apologetically.

'It's OK. How long was I sleeping?' I get slightly dizzy as I try to sit up.

'About an hour. I brought you rehydration solution, some coconut water, pretzels, and chicken soup.'

'That's so sweet of you.' I guess he must have some experiences with food poisoning because this is exactly what you need the next day or two.

He reaches into the grocery bag. ‘Here’s the chicken soup.’

He puts the chicken soup on the table. I sit upright and eat only a couple of spoons, not knowing if it is going to stay in me or if it’s going to make me rush to the toilet. David goes into the kitchen and comes back with a glass of water and a bowl of pretzels.

‘And here are some pretzels and the rehydration solution. You should drink it slowly.’

He puts them on the table and sits down next to me.

‘Yes, mum.’ I try to smile as I say it, but I can only manage a weak smile.

‘I guess seafood is off the menu for a while.’

I nod.

‘Whenever I had a stomach bug, my mum would make me chicken and rice. Do you think you could eat that?’

The thought of food makes me nauseous. ‘Maybe in a couple of hours. I think I have some chicken in the freezer, let me just defrost it.’

I try to get up, but David puts his hand on my knee.

‘Don’t be silly, you stay here and rest, and I will make you lunch.’

‘You don’t have to do that. It will just take a minute and I will rest then.’ I am half standing at this point.

'Don't be silly.' He takes my hand and gently pulls me down on the sofa. 'You're not used to someone take care of you, now are you?'

He's right.

'When you've lived on your own for a while, you get used to doing things yourself, no matter how sick you are.'

I don't get sick very often, and when I do, I just deal with it on my own. When I lived with my sister, she used to move out for that time so she wouldn't catch anything. When the roles were reversed, I always stayed with her and nursed her back to health just because I know it really makes a difference.

'Well, you have me here. You took care of me when Rob moved out, now let me take care of you.'

Ah, bless his soul! And he fully delivers – I can't remember the last time I was this pampered, it almost makes being ill fun. I am back on my feet by the time it's time to go to work.

Chapter 14

The school bell rings and pupils run out of the classroom. Petra appears at the door of my classroom, visibly tired.

'Oh man, I can't wait for Christmas to be over.'

I'm surprised at her statement, so I say, 'I thought you liked Christmas.'

'I do, I do, but there are just so many things to do here at school, and then I spend the afternoons running around like crazy to buy supplies and gifts, going out on dates …'

'Ah, you love going out on dates, admit it.' She does. She finds flirting fun.

'It's fun, but some of the men I've been out with already want me to spend New Year's Eve with them, and I'm like 'Relax, this is only our first date. I don't know if I like you that much that I am willing to let you be my first kiss in the new year.'

I smile. I guess New Year's Eve and Valentine's Day make people want to be in a relationship even more and they get into one much faster than at other times of the year.

'What are we going to do about you?' she asks.

Because I have no idea what she is talking about, so I answer with a question, 'What do you mean?'

'We need to find you a man.'

'Oh, that again.' I guess she doesn't understand that I don't find dating fun.

‘Can you blame me if I want you to be happy?’ she asks.

‘I don’t need a man to be happy.’ Ugh, that sounded a bit harsh.

She quickly corrects herself and says, ‘OK, then happily in love.’

I say, ‘You know I don’t fall in love easily.’ It’s partially true. I don’t find many men attractive, so it takes me a bit more time than the average person to find someone who makes my heart race, but at the same time I can fall in love with someone that I find attractive quite fast. I think it’s the energy they exude that pulls me in.

‘And when you do, you go for the wrong men.’

I object, ‘No, I don’t.’

She puts her hands on her hips and says, ‘Really? Remember Michael, your college crush?’

‘Yes.’ Damn.

She continues, ‘He only started going for coffee with you when he saw you make great notes.’

I start defending him, ‘Hey, maybe he wanted to get to know me first before he …’, but I am cut off.

‘And he stopped calling you as soon as college was over.’

‘Hey!’ I am slightly hurt.

She goes on.

‘And then there was Andrew, the Art teacher who worked here for a year.’

More salt to my wound. As if the first one didn't sting enough. I say quietly, 'Maybe he just didn't like me like that.' My voice trembles.

'Tina, please,' she objects. 'You could see it in his eyes that he liked you.'

I let out a sigh when I say, 'Well, he wasn't over his ex.'

'It could be, but that didn't stop him from asking you out, and when he got your attention and your heart, he just pulled away. You told me yourself that he never called you after he stopped working here.'

All I can do is sigh again.

'And then there was Matt ...'

'OK, I get it,' I say slightly annoyed. She's right, but I am still annoyed. No one likes their faults to be laid out.

She says, 'You seem to go for the unavailable ones.'

I think for a second and reply, 'I guess I do.'

I think that's the end of our conversation about my love life, but she continues, 'It's the same with David now. You know he's gay and that you can never be together, but you spend a lot of time with him.'

'But I like him.' What's wrong with spending time with people you like? I also spend time with her and she doesn't have a problem with that.

She comes to me and takes my hand.

'Don't get me wrong. I like it that he is helping you with your issues, but, honey, you need someone to hold your hand and hug you and kiss you in a romantic way.'

Bam - straight into my heart.

I guess I look really upset because she starts apologizing, 'Sorry, that was not my intention,' and gives me a hug. She continues, 'You need to put yourself out there, show them that you are available. You need to go out and meet men, men who will adore you and treat you right, and then pick the one who worships the ground you walk on.'

I smile a bit and ask her, 'Have you been drinking?' This is a whole different side of Petra. She's never been so direct.

She offers some more words of wisdom and says, 'You need to open your heart to love again, and when you do, love will come to you.'

I sigh and say, 'I wish it were this easy.'

'Sometimes you just need to make the first step. Promise me you will spend a bit less time with David and open your eyes to what else is out there.'

I nod.

As we are leaving the classroom, I know that Petra is right. Ever since I was young, I would always have a crush or fall in love with either shy men who wouldn't pluck up the courage to ask me out, and since I'm also shy, the relationships were doomed before they even started, or I'd fall in love with those who didn't even know I existed or just didn't see me as anything but a friend. Being around David has helped me realize that I could have a meaningful relationship with a man, and that a man's touch can feel soothing, but once again I am falling for someone who can't be with me.

Chapter 15

The last few weeks have gone by really fast and it's only one week until the New Year. I've been baking the whole day today for Christmas dinner at David's. I've even managed to buy everyone a small present.

It's the usual gang – Ian, Howard, Emma, and Mark. We've hung out a few times since Activity night – we celebrated Howard's birthday in November, went out for dinner, and we even went paintballing. Needless to say Emma and I were the first ones eliminated, but we didn't mind that. Oh, we also had a karaoke night – that was so much fun! I don't think I've ever laughed so hard. The guys decided to accompany their singing with heart-felt emotions and acting out the lyrics. I was laughing so hard I started crying.

But tonight will be a bit more peaceful. We have just finished eating and you can see that everyone enjoyed the food because there's hardly anything left.

Ian taps his belly a few times and says, 'Dinner was delicious.'

'It's nice to have us as your friends, isn't it, Ian?' Emma teases.

'Hey, I can cook,' he replies with a defiant tone. 'Just not as good as the rest of you,' he adds and smiles.

Seeing that everyone has finished eating, I ask, 'Do you have room for dessert?' and I get a 'Yes' from everyone.

'OK, let me get it,' I stand up and go into the kitchen.

I hear David say, 'And I'll just clear the table.'

Good thinking because I need some empty place to put the dessert plates on.

I immediately start cutting the banana roll and put slices on plates. David comes in, puts the dirty dishes into the sink, then stands next to me and asks if he can help.

Carrying one plate in one hand is the best I can do without food falling on the floor, so I accept his help and hand him two plates with a slice of banana roll and a few rum balls. Just as he grabs hold of them, Emma comes into the kitchen, looks at us and says, 'OK, both of you stand still.'

David looks at her worried and asks, 'Why? What's wrong?'

'You two are standing under the mistletoe and you know what that means,' she explains.

David and I look up. There is a mistletoe hanging from the light above our heads.

'Who put this up here?' David asks.

'I did,' Emma proudly replies. She takes a few steps towards David and says, 'Now let me take these off your hands.' Before David or I can say anything, she takes the two plates from David and says, 'There's nothing in your way now. Go ahead.'

We kiss quickly and think that's it, but Emma objects, 'Oh, come on. That was terrible. That's how you kiss your aunt or uncle. You can do better. Now do it right, otherwise you will have bad sex for years.'

'I'm pretty sure that is true for not looking into the other person's eyes during a toast,' David replies.

Before she leaves the kitchen, Emma says, 'Anyway, make it believable this time. The universe is watching.'

Do I even have to say I am nervous? I can feel my heart beating like crazy, and I am pretty sure you can hear it, too. I try to calm myself down with saying 'It's only a pretend kiss, it means nothing' to myself, but it doesn't seem to do much.

He turns towards me. This is probably like a routine for him – he is used to kissing women without any feelings involved. He is an actor, after all.

I have no idea what to do – should I put my hands around his neck, should I place them on his chest, or should I not touch him at all?

I don't know if he can see that I am panicking, but I guess he doesn't because he doesn't say a word, he just puts his left hand on my waist and pulls me close. I place my right hand on his arm and my left arm rests on his chest. With his right hand he gently caresses my cheek, slowly leans in and gives me a soft, yet passionate kiss. I think I stop breathing for a few seconds.

When the kiss is over, we slowly pull away. After a moment of silence, I start saying the first thing that comes to my mind, 'Hmm, I think …,' and I have to stop and cough slightly because my voice seems high and trembly, and then I continue, '… we better bring these to the hungry masses.' I point at the slices of banana roll.

He lets go of me and replies, 'Hm.' I take it as a 'Yes.'

We enter the dining room and I keep my head down, avoiding eye contact with anyone in the room, especially Emma, just in case my eyes say what my heart feels.

Luckily, the others don't pay special attention to us, their focus seems to go to the banana roll and the rum balls David and I place on the table.

When we finish eating, Howard suggests we go to the bar. Mark adds, 'I hear it's quiz night tonight.'

Emma is excited and says, 'I've always wanted to do that.'

Half an hour later we are sitting in the bar. I sit down next to David but just because this means less eye contact than if we were sitting opposite each other.

A man is standing on the stage and he is reading out the questions. So far, we're only unsure about one of our answers, which means we have a shot at getting a free round.

The man says, 'Question 10. Yeomen Warders of Her Majesty's Royal Palace and Fortress the Tower of London are better known as what?'

Mark and I whisper, 'Beefeaters.' at the same time and start smiling at each other.

David is surprised that we know the answer and asks us how we know it, to which Mark replies, 'I know my gin.' I know it because I took a tour around the Tower of London a few years ago.

The host says, 'This concludes round one. Please, bring your answers to me. Round two will begin in ten minutes.'

I stand up and take the paper with our answers to him. As I am waiting in line to hand our answers in, I discretely observe our table. I see that Ian and David are talking, and I think they are talking about me because I can see both look at me at one point.

Once I've handed in our answers, I go over to the counter to order another round for our table. Ian comes over.

He starts the conversation with, 'I'm glad David has such smart people as his friends. I like getting free things.'

I smile at him, and he continues, 'Even if that means that I have to lose at Activity every now and then.'

I guess that was quite a shock to him. I smile again.

He seems to become slightly nervous. Is it because I haven't said anything and just smiled? But it isn't. He continues, 'Listen. I was … er … wondering if you'd like to get a drink sometimes. Just the two of us.'

This is not what I was expecting. I mean, we've had fun together, but I didn't get the vibe from him, telling me that he wants to be more than friends with me. My eyes immediately look at David and I see him looking at us. When he sees I am looking at him, he smiles and turns his head to Howard. So they were talking about me a minute ago! Did Ian tell David he wanted to ask me out? What did David say?

And then Petra's voice appears in my head and says, 'Tina, David and you are just friends, and that is all you'll ever be. Stop obsessing over him and find your happiness somewhere else. Give men a chance.'

It hits me like a ton of bricks, but that's just what I needed. A reality check. A wake-up call. I look at Ian and say, 'Sure.'

He takes out his mobile and puts in my phone number. The waiter brings the drinks, I pay, and we return to our table. Round two is a success and we win the quiz. We spend another hour in the pub and then we head home.

Just as we are saying goodbye outside in the street, David's phone rings. He looks at it and when he sees who is calling, he say, 'Excuse me for a second.'

He takes a few steps away from the group and answers the phone. A minute later he joins us. Emma sees he looks strange and asks him what's wrong. He tells us he got a lead. We are all very excited and congratulate him, but he still looks a bit strange.

Emma comments, 'You don't seem thrilled.'

I ask him, 'What's the catch?'

David surprises us when he replies, 'I leave for London the day after tomorrow.'

Emma is amazed and says, 'Wow, London! I've always wanted to go there. Can I come with you?'

Ian asks, 'How long will you be there for?' to which David replies, 'My agent said 6 weeks.'

Emma is still excited when she says, 'So you'll be singing Auld Lang Syne along the banks of the Thames next week.'

I don't say a thing. While I am happy that he's finally got that break, I can only think about the fact that he will be gone for six long weeks. That's until the beginning of February. That's long! Too long.

Chapter 16

The day of his departure has arrived. I go over to say goodbye. When he opens the door, I hand him a bag with chocolate chip cookies, and say, ‘I thought you might like these.’

He thanks me and puts them into his backpack. I look around his living room and say, ‘I see you’re packed and ready to go.’

‘Yup. Taxi is picking me up in five minutes.’ He seems a bit distant. I am not used to seeing him like this.

I offer to come with him to the airport, but he says, ‘Better not. I really hate goodbyes, so it’s best to just do them quickly.’

I make a sad face and I say, ‘I’m really going to miss you.’

This seems to turn him into the affectionate David that I know because he opens his arms, says, ‘Come here!’ and hugs me. He adds, ‘And I’m going to miss you.’

We stay in an embrace for a few seconds.

‘Thanks god for Internet,’ he says.

‘Yeah, but you’ll be working all the time. And then there’s the time difference.’

‘Don’t worry. Besides, you still have your friends and …’

And then I realize that he’ll be in London all alone.

‘Oh, you’ll be all alone. Now I’m really sad.’

I guess he’s already given this a thought because he replies immediately, ‘Then it’s a good thing I’ll be working long days.’

I try to be encouraging and say, ‘And who knows, maybe someone catches your eye.’

David smiles and says, ‘I don’t know about that.’

I still want to lift his sprits and say enthusiastically, ‘Hey, you never know. You might come back a married man.’

He starts laughing out loud and says, ‘I thought goodbyes were supposed to be sad.’

We can hear a horn honk and David says, ‘I think that’s my taxi.’

‘I’ll help you carry your things down.’

We go downstairs in complete silence. The taxi driver puts David’s suitcases into the trunk of the car, so it’s time for our final goodbyes.

All I can say is, ‘Have a safe flight. And an amazing time in London.’

‘You too.’

We hug, and then David drives off in the taxi. I look at the taxi as it’s driving away and my heart is filled with sadness.

I fly to my sisters’ the next day and spending 5 days with them and my nieces and nephews brings a smile on my face. I’m glad I have them, especially during the holidays. These can be quite hard if you are single and you live hundreds of miles from your family.

I’m back home a day after the New Year. I’ve just put the dirty clothes into the washing machine, and I am sitting at the computer, reading the news to see if I’ve missed something important. Just as I am about to get myself some chocolate, I get a call on Skype.

It's David. I answer the call with a big grin and an excited wave.

'Happy New Year! How's London?'

'Happy New Year to you, too. Well, I haven't had much time for sightseeing. We've been working non-stop, and I think jet leg is setting in. Today is my first day off and I slept for 12 hours.'

'Wow, you must have been really …. Wait, what's the word ….' I stop and think for a second, and then I put on my best British accent and say, '… knackered.'

David laughs, then adds, 'I'm sure I'll be fine in a few days'.

A thought comes into my mind and I have to share it before I forget it, so I say, 'Hey, you never told me what the movie was about.'

'It's a romantic comedy. It's actually the one you helped me prepare for the audition.'

I put on my serious face and say, 'In that case I think I should get some royalty.'

'We can negotiate,' he says with a smile. It's nice to see him back to his old self.

'Oh, or some blueberry muffins. I love them. I think I ate four a day when I was in London a few years ago.' Just thinking of them makes my mouth water. They were so fluffy and moist at the same time, which is kind of hard to achieve.

'I'll see what I can do about it,' he says.

We talk for about an hour, and then I let him catch up on his sleep. It might be early afternoon here, but it's already time to go to bed in London.

I get a phone call from Ian a bit later, asking me if we are still on for this evening. I almost forgot about it! I tell him we are and he tells me he is picking me up at seven.

We play pool and then we have dinner. I don't feel any butterflies in my stomach when he touches me or when he looks at me. Maybe I am just a bit tired from all the activities with my sisters and their children and getting up early today to catch my 9 o'clock flight, so I decide to go out with him a couple more times in the next days, but by the third date we both know that this isn't it. Don't get me wrong, he is still an amazing person with a great sense of humor, but he's just not the right one for me. In fact, I think he and Petra would really hit it off, so I introduce them and I was right. They get on like a house on fire, and by the time Ian's birthday comes along, they are a couple.

We're celebrating his birthday at his place. He's had a couple of glasses of wine so he is a bit tipsy when he comes over to me. He says, 'Here you are! The woman who's made me the happiest man on Earth.'

While he is hugging me, I correct him, 'I think Petra is that woman.'

'I'm a bit drunk,' he says, 'but you know what I mean. Now, let's take a selfie.' He wraps his arm around me, raises his phone, and then gives me a friendly kiss on the check as he takes a photo. He shows it to me and when I say it looks great, he posts it on Facebook and writes 'The reason for my happiness' and adds a smiley face.

Chapter 17

I throw myself into work and sport for the next few weeks. I talk to David a few times, but the time difference and him working every day make it difficult. He does tell me the day of him returning home and I decide to surprise him and make him some delicious food. He has told me quite a few times that the British food is not his cup of tea and that he would do anything for a home-cooked meal.

So, here I am, talking to Petra on the phone and carrying a grocery bag. She suggest we go out dancing tonight, but I reply, 'You know I'd love to come out with you tonight, but David is coming back this afternoon and I want to catch up.'

'You can both come,' she suggests.

I tell her I'll ask him and will let her know. He might be too tired after a long journey. I know I would be.

I come to his apartment, unlock the door, and enter. He gave me his keys so that I could water the plants. I head towards the kitchen when David comes out of the bathroom, wearing only his boxer shorts, and drying his hair with a towel.

He scares the crap out of me (pardon my French), so I scream and drop the grocery bag onto the floor. Some food falls out of the bag.

I place one hand on chest and say, 'Oh my god, you scared me.'

I am still recovering from the shock when he comes over and gives me a hug. I hug him back. I can see he's lost some weight and I can feel it, too. He must have been working really hard and forgot to eat regularly.

I ask, 'What are you doing here? Weren't you supposed to come in a couple of hours?'

'I wanted to surprise you, so I caught an earlier flight.'

'That sure was some surprise. And I wanted to surprise you and make you dinner,' I say and look down at the grocery bag. I kneel down and start picking up the food on the floor. It's a welcome distraction from his abs. Don't get me wrong – his abs look amazing, but my eyes keep going there and they shouldn't. Daydreaming about his chiseled body won't get me anywhere.

'I'm dying for a home-cooked meal. I'll help you, just let me put some clothes on.'

He goes into his bedroom, and I go into the kitchen and start preparing dinner. He comes about a minute later with a wrapped gift in his hands. He says, 'I hope these are the right ones.'

I quickly open it and I see blueberry muffins.

'You remembered!' I say and do a happy dance. 'Thank you, thank you, thank you!' I add and give him a hug. As you can see I am really, really excited. 'Aren't they the most delicious food you've ever had?' I ask him.

'I haven't tried them yet. I thought I'd try them with someone who adores them,' he says and smiles. 'That is if you can spare a bite.'

'Sure. I mean what's a bite when I have tree whole muffins and some left,' I say with a cheeky grin.

I open the package and cut one muffin in half. I hand him his half, and then I take my half and smell it. Correction – I don't just smell it, I inhale it.

'I've never met someone who would enjoy food so much,' he says, 'and that's even before they taste it.' He takes a bite and gives his verdict. 'Hmm, oh my God, these are delicious.'

'You see, I told you so. I think I should take the rest into my apartment otherwise they will be gone before lunch.' I take two muffins out of the package and take them to my apartment. I leave one for him – it's only fair, especially after he said he liked them.

When I return, we continue cooking and I ask him to tell me everything about London.

'Well, I didn't have much free time, so I only saw the sights from the hop-on-hop-off bus. On days off I would just catch up on my sleep and then hang out with some of the cast.'

'And, did you meet anyone special?' I ask carefully but with a smile.

'No.'

I don't give up on the subject and continue, 'Come on, I'm sure there was someone who got your heart rate up?'

He laughs and replies, 'I'm telling the truth. Speaking of finding someone special, I see that Ian and you are getting pretty close.'

'We just went on a couple of dates,' I say calmly.

'His Facebook photos tell a different story.'

‘What are you talking about?’ Yes, what is he talking about?

David takes out his phone and shows me the photo he had in mind.

‘Ah, this one!’ I say. ‘We’re just friends. The only reason he is kissing me on the cheek is because he was thanking me for introducing him to Petra.’

I can see that he is surprised. I guess it isn’t the answer he was expecting. He only says, ‘Oh.’

I explain a bit more, ‘He’s a nice guy but there just wasn’t any spark between us. After getting to know him better, I just thought that he’d be perfect for Petra, so I set them up.’

Just as he is about to say something, the doorbell rings. He says excitedly, ‘Maybe it’s the airport with my luggage.’

He goes out of the kitchen. I can hear him talk to someone, and a few seconds later he opens the kitchen door. I turn my head away from the stove and I see that there’s an older couple coming into the kitchen after him.

David says, ‘Tina, these are my mum and dad.’

I wipe my hand into a tablecloth, then take a few steps towards David’s parents with my hand extended.

David turns to his mum and dad and says, ‘And this is Tina.’

David’s mum says, ‘Your girlfriend.’

I am surprised at her statement. I start objecting and say, ‘Oh, I …’

But I am cut off before I can finish. David's mum says, 'David's told us so much about you. It's nice to finally meet you.'

Before I can say anything his mum gives me a hug.

Then David's dad shakes my hand and we say 'Nice to meet you' to each other.

I am surprised that David doesn't say anything about his mum's assumption. But what surprises me even more is that he comes to me and puts his arm around me. Like in slow motion, I look at his hand around my shoulder and then at David.

He doesn't look at me, he just says to his parents, 'Mum, Dad, you must be tired after a long journey. Why don't you go and make yourselves comfortable in the dining room and I will bring you something to drink.'

When David's mum and dad go into dining room, I turn to David and whisper, 'Your girlfriend? Why would they think I was your girlfriend?'

David whispers back, 'I don't know.'

'And why didn't you correct them?' I am slightly annoyed, but because we are still whispering I don't think it was conveyed.

'I just can't bear for them to ask me when I am going to get a girlfriend one more time.'

His answer surprises me. 'Oh, so they don't …'

Before I can finish what I wanted to say, we can hear David's mum from the dining room say, 'Honey, if you have chamomile tea, that would be perfect.'

I turn back to David and he is clasping hands together as if praying and he whispers, 'Please, please, please do this for me.'

'I don't know. I'm terrible with parents. I get nervous and …'

'Just be yourself, they'll love you.'

'I don't know, David.' Dealing with parents is nerve-racking. Especially when they think I am his girlfriend.

David begs, 'It's just for one afternoon. Please.'

I think about it and then I give in, 'Well, you have helped me, so it's only fair I help you.' Even when I am saying it, I am thinking 'What have I got myself into?'

He whispers, 'Thank you, thank you,' and then he takes my face into his hands and kisses me on the lips. He says 'Thank you' again.

When lunch is ready, I bring it into the dining room. I confess, I was kind of hiding in the kitchen, trying to gather up the courage and praying everything will be fine, but now it's time to face the music.

Lunch goes over well, but that's only because David talks about London and his parents about their cruise. I clear the table when we are finished, sit down next to David, and after a while I start nervously tapping my fingers on the chair. David notices that and puts his hand gently over mine, gently caressing it, and then lets his hand rest on mine. I stop tapping my fingers, look down, and then over to David. He looks at me and smiles lovingly, so I blush and smile back.

David's mum notices this and says, 'It must have been really hard being away from each other for so long.'

I blush even more, then I look at David and I see he is blushing as well. Probably from feeling guilty about lying to his parents. We only respond with 'Hmmm.'

David's mum continues, 'Especially at the beginning of a relationship when you just want to spend every minute with the person you love.'

Just when I thought it couldn't get more awkward.

David says, 'Mum!' in a tone that lets her know that he is feeling embarrassed.

'What?' his mum replies. 'I remember what that is like.'

David looks at me and says, 'I apologize for this.'

I actually find it quite funny. Maybe because it's the first time I see David feel uncomfortable, he's otherwise so composed.

They want to know more about me, so I tell them the basics about my family, my upbringing, my job and my passions. Things get a bit more complicated when they ask about our relationship. Since I am not good at lying, and because he got us into this mess, I let David do the talking. He doesn't tell them about the healing project, which I am grateful for, he just says we spent a lot of time together and that's how we grew closer and one thing led to another. Before she gets to dig deeper, she gets a phone call from a friend.

'Oh, it's Betsy. I've completely forgotten that we are meeting her today. I guess I was just so excited about seeing my baby after a long time,' she says and goes into the living room to answer the call. When she returns, she tells us they have to leave because Betsy is picking them up in five minutes.

We walk them to the elevator, and as we are saying goodbye, she tells David, 'I think this is the happiest I've seen you in a long time, so don't mess it up this time. She's a keeper. You just look so cute together it warms my heart.'

David blushes and says, 'I'll try my best.'

She then turns to me and says, 'I'm so happy I've finally met you. I hope we can become good friends. And if this one causes any trouble,' she points at him when she says it, 'just phone me.'

I have to smile – I mean, just imagine a 20-something man being scolded by his mother!

The elevator comes. Just as they are about to step into it, his mum says, 'Oh, I've just had an idea. Let me take a photo of the cute couple!' and takes out her mobile phone.

David wraps his right hand around my waist, but because I wasn't expecting this, I slightly lose my balance and only catch it when I put my right hand on his chest. I think my left hand lands on his behind. He doesn't seem to mind, he just holds me tightly and we pose for the camera. His mum looks at the photo, says, 'Perfect! I'll send it to you!' and then we say goodbye.

The elevator door closes and David and I turn around to go back to the apartment. After a couple of seconds I say, 'You know you will have to come clean to your parents one day?'

‘I know, I know, and I’m sorry I dragged you into this, but I just couldn’t take my mum asking me when I was going to get a girlfriend one more time.’

‘I mean, wouldn’t it be easier if you just came out to them? Just tell them you’re gay and then you can live your life …’

David stops, gives me a surprised look and says, ‘I’m not gay. Why would you think I was?’

I’m equally as surprised and explain, ‘Well, because you lived with Robbie, and you felt down when he moved out. And whenever either of you left home, you’d say ‘I love you’ to each other.’

He smiles when he says, ‘Tina, Rob is my brother.’

Brother? Brother!? I’m trying to wrap my head around this information.

He continues, ‘Of course I was sad when he moved out because he is my best friend and he took Goldie with him. I was sad that I wouldn’t see him and Goldie every day anymore.’

I’m still visibly in shock.

He goes on, ‘And the reason why we always said ‘I love you’ to each other was because my mum insisted on it. You see, she lost her sister when she was young. They had a fight, and later that day her sister was hit by a drunk driver and she died. My mum felt terrible and she regretted not telling her sister she loved her, so she made sure that we would always tell each other that when we left home.’

All I can say is, 'Oh, I feel so embarrassed now. I mean, you two always looked close, and because you don't look alike I just assumed that you were a couple.'

Then the information starts to sink in and my mind starts working overtime. Words come out before I am able to process them, 'So, when we were holding hands, and went to dance lessons, and when we were hugging, you weren't gay?'

I don't hear what his response is, I just continue, 'And I told you about my fears and I shared very personal information with you … Oh, this is bad.' I start hyperventilating. I hear him ask me if I am OK, but I just say, 'Oh, God, I feel so embarrassed. I think I need a few days … I'm sorry, I can't. I just can't.'

I see he doesn't get what I am trying to say, but I can't deal with that at this moment. I go into my apartment and lock the door. I hear him knock on the door and call my name, but I just rush into the bathroom and try to calm myself by splashing cold water on my face and let it run on my wrists.

How could I not see it? We spent all this time together and I didn't notice? But he never talked about ex-girlfriends, he never made any comments about women we'd see on the street, I don't think I saw him look at a woman the way men do when they find her attractive. The reason why I never brought up his sexuality is because I didn't want him to feel sad when he'd think about Rob, and because he never brought him up, I just thought that he didn't want to talk about him because it hurt him too much.

I pace around my bathroom for quite some time and I cannot calm down, so I decide to phone Petra and ask her if I can spend the next few days at her place. I am relieved when she says 'Yes'.

I pack up all of the essentials and I go to her place.

Chapter 18

It's now been a couple of days later. Petra and I are in her kitchen. We are preparing material for Valentine's Day for school – we are cutting out hearts and Cupids. I know, not the best activity for me at this time, but today the head teacher decided it would be nice if we also decorate the halls, so the teachers had to step up. Thank God, Valentine's Day is tomorrow because I don't think I could stand one more day cutting out hearts.

My phone starts ringing. I look at who is calling me, and then I press the 'ignore' button that sends the caller straight to voice mail.

Petra sees this and says, 'You know you're going to have to talk to him eventually.'

'I know. I just can't do it today.' I don't know how long I can keep this up, but I'm still torn inside. 'It's getting late. Can you do the last few?' I ask her and when she nods, I say, 'I'll just take a shower.'

I always think clear when I am having a shower. I've had some of my best ideas while showering and I hope this one will bring clarity. I think I hear my phone while I am in the shower, but I only hear it ring for a brief moment, so it might just be in my head. I hear Petra talking – I guess she is talking to Ian. Maybe it was her phone I heard and since I am in the shower, I didn't hear correctly and thought it was mine. She comes close to the bathroom a minute later and says, 'Hey, listen, I'm just going to see Ian for about an hour.'

I tell her to have fun.

As I am putting on clothes, I think about what a bad friend I've been these past days. I haven't asked Petra about her and Ian, and now she has to sneak out of her own apartment to be with him. I decide to apologize when she comes home, but I don't get a chance because I only get a text from her, saying she is spending the night at Ian's.

The opportunity comes the next day when we come home from work. We are sitting on the sofa in the living room and I say, 'I'm really sorry. I've been a really bad friend. I've not said much and I haven't even asked you about you and Ian. How's it going?'

She gushes over him and I am very happy that they're happy together. I say, 'Listen, if you have plans for tonight and want me to leave, just tell me, I'll understand. I mean, it is Valentine's.'

Much to my surprise she says, 'Don't worry about it. We spent yesterday evening together and decided that I am spending Valentine's with you.'

'But won't he feel lonely?' I ask.

'He'll be with David,' she answers. 'He's been rather down lately.'

I look down in shame, knowing that I am to blame.

'So, are you going to tell me what's he done that makes you behave like this?' she asks.

We haven't talked about it yet. When I came over, I just said that I needed a couple of days away. She's known me for a long time now, so she knows when to just leave me alone and let me mull over whatever's bothering me. But she also knows that I am over-analytical and that in such cases I need a voice of reason to get me out of the hole I dug out for myself. I guess she thinks this is such an occasion.

I say, 'Promise you won't laugh at me or be judgmental or …,' I'm trying to find the right word, but my mind is too tired, so I just say, 'whatever. Just listen to me. And it doesn't make sense to me, so I don't expect it will make any sense to you.'

She only says, 'OK.'

I try to explain the situation to the best of my abilities. I start with, 'David isn't gay.'

She says, 'But I thought you'd be happy about it.'

'And so did I,' I say. 'But then it hit me. He knows everything about me. And I mean *everything*. He knows things not even you know. I mean, I thought he was gay and I opened up to him. I don't do that. I don't tell you or my sisters everything, let alone a man. But it seemed different in my mind with him, I didn't see him as a man if you know what I mean, and I shared my heart and soul with him. I felt safe around him because he posed no threat. That's why I agreed to holding hands with him and dancing and hugging.'

Petra stops my stream of thoughts and asks, 'Has he ever stepped over the line while you were doing your experiment?'

'No, never.'

'You see, he only had good intentions. And now he knows you for who you really are. He knows your secrets and fears, he's seen your flaws and your beautiful soul, and he is still around.'

‘True.’ I see her point but fear still cripples me. ‘But I've never let a man see that side of me before.’

‘That's what you do when you are in a relationship, and I don't mean just boyfriend and girlfriend relationship. Friends do that, too.’

I sigh. I know I have a hard time letting people in.

She continues, ‘And now you can be you, no pretenses. Isn't that liberating?’

‘Hmm.’ I think about whether I feel liberated.

‘Tina, don't let a good man walk out of your life because of your insecurities. Especially insecurities that are only there in your mind.’

Are they really only in my mind? And how am I going to explain all of this to David? And where do we go from here?

‘Now, let’s get ready for dinner. Is it OK if I have a shower first?’ she asks.

‘Sure, no problem.’ She always puts make up on when we go out, so it’s best she showers first and then she can do all the girlie things while I am in the shower.

Just as we are about to leave the apartment, she asks, ‘Oh, may I borrow that perfume of yours?’

‘Oh, I left it at the apartment, I’m sorry. I didn’t think I’d need it while staying at your place.’

She looks disappointed. ‘Oh, no, I really love it. Let’s just stop by your place and you can take it.’

I open my mouth to say something, but Petra beats me to it and says, 'He won't be there, remember? I talked to Ian while you were getting ready, and he and David are already commiserating. Now, let us girls have some fun!'

We leave the apartment. The taxi is on time and we ask the taxi driver to make a quick stop at my place.

I hear her say, 'Thank you for doing this.'

We step out of the taxi and walk into the building. I ask Petra if she is sure David isn't at home, and she takes out her mobile from her purse, shows me a photo of him and Ian and says, 'See?!'

I walk quietly as a mouse towards my apartment. I glance over at David's and I feel a knot in my stomach. I quickly take the keys out of my purse and unlock the door, leaving the keys in the lock. We enter, leaving the door open. I go into my bathroom and a few seconds later I exit, carrying a perfume bottle in her hands. I lift it up as I am entering the living room and say, 'Here it is.'

But when enter the living room, I see that David is standing nervously next to Petra.

I am surprised and nervous at the same time. I look at Petra and open my mouth but I don't know what to say.

Petra looks at us and says, 'You two need to talk.'

She turns around, ready to leave the apartment. She stops at the door and turns around.

'This was all my idea, so don't be angry at him,' she says, leaves the apartment and locks the door.

Damn, I shouldn't have left the keys in the lock. Now I can't escape. I hear her say something but she isn't talking to us. Aha! She must have had an accomplice! I bet it was Ian.

I look at David and I've never been this nervous in my life. If you combine the nerves I felt before and during each phase of the healing process and multiply it by ten, you might get a fraction of what I am feeling right now.

I don't know how to start, so I blurt out, 'Can I offer you something to drink?' and then kind of whisper to myself, 'I sure need something.'

You see, I'm so nervous that I even think about having some alcohol to calm me down!

David says he's fine, but I head into the kitchen. David follows me. Only then do I remember that I don't have any alcohol because I never drink it, so I pour myself a glass of water and take a few sips. I turn around to face David. He is standing a few steps away from me.

David nervously starts the conversation, 'I'm really sorry about the whole situation. I honestly didn't know that you thought I was gay.'

It's time to let him know it wasn't his fault, so I say, 'It's mostly my fault. I mean, I saw Rob and you be affectionate to each other and I just assumed that you were a couple. And then when he moved out, I didn't want to ask any questions or bring him up in conversation because I didn't want to make you feel uncomfortable or sad.'

'Oh.'

I go on, 'Because I thought you were gay, it was so easy to open up to you. The tension that I would normally feel around men was gone. I mean, I did have some reservations, but you just made it so easy for me to share my thoughts, my feelings, and my fears. And then when I found out you weren't gay, it just made me feel … ashamed.'

'Ashamed? But why? You have nothing to be ashamed about,' he says in the most reassuring voice and takes a few steps towards me.

'I know, it's just that I've never let anyone in as much as I let you. I told you things about me that not even my friends and family know about. Things that people usually keep to themselves,' I say with a trembling voice.

'And it didn't make me run away,' he says. He takes a step closer and continues, 'So please don't run away from me.'

There is a moment of silence.

I am overcome with emotion because of what he's just sad. I can hear my voice crack when I ask, 'Why? Why did you help me?'

He replies in a soothing voice, 'It's what people do when they care for each other. You helped me when Rob moved out and I wanted to be there for you like you were there for me. Besides, everyone has their insecurities. It's what makes us human. And all I wanted was to help you overcome them.'

I take a deep breath.

He continues, 'And the way you faced them, how you handled them made me proud of you and admire you.'

No one's ever told me they were proud of me or that they admired me. I blush and look down for a second. Then I look at him and say, 'Well, I couldn't have done it without your help.'

He takes another step towards me, so that he is less than a feet away. He takes a deep breath and says, 'And it has made me love you even more.'

I look at him, puzzled. I try to read his face expression. Did he mean that he loves me like a friend or more than a friend? He looks nervous, but then he lifts his right hand and with a trembling hand he caresses my left cheek. I feel relief go through my body, I close my eyes for a second and just enjoy his caress. My eyes fill with tears, and when I open them, I give him a smile. He smiles back, and then he slowly leans in and we kiss. Softly. Passionately.

Emotions get the best of me, so when the kiss is over, I hug him. I hold him really tight. Like it's our last hug. And then I cry. I let go of all the past disappointments, all the past heartbreaks.

When I'm almost done with crying, he whispers 'I love you' into my ear. I start smiling and then the smile turns into a laugh. I am happy. Completely happy. I look at him and say with the biggest smile, 'I love you, too.'

www.ingramcontent.com/pod-product-compliance
Lightning Source LLC
Chambersburg PA
CBHW072231190626
46809CB00017B/1694